NEMESIS

Brian Venables

This book is a work of fiction and except in the case of historical facts, any resemblance to actual persons living or dead is purely coincidental.

© Brian Venables 2020

The rights of Brian Venables to be identified as the author of this work have been asserted by him in accordance with the Copyright, Designs and Patents Act of 1988.

All rights reserved; no part of this publication may be reproduced, stored in a retrieval system, or transmitted in any form or by any means, electronic, mechanical, photocopying, recording or otherwise without the prior written consent of the publisher or a licence permitting copying in the UK issued by the Copyright Licensing Agency Ltd. www.cla.co.uk

ISBN 978-1-78222-810-3

Book design, layout and production management by Into Print
www.intoprint.net
+44 (0)1604 832149

1

The wind and rain battered against the windows of the old cottage. For over two hundred years it had stood in the shelter of a small hill on the North Yorkshire Moors. Guy sipped his coffee in the kitchen warmed by the aga cooker as he watched the news on TV.

There had been another terrorist attack in Brussels railway station, five dead including the bomber.

He sighed at the scene before his eyes; when would it ever stop?

Guy was no stranger to either the bombers or indeed the terrorists, he had finished his third tour of Afghanistan just seven months before. He had served as a Flt/Lt, in the RAF Regiment for the past fifteen years, during which time he had been wounded whilst on patrol. He could remember the feeling like being hit with a sledgehammer, he had been lucky – or so he was told by the doctor. It had been a round from a sniper, known as a through and through, no damaged bone or major arteries the bullet exiting just below his right shoulder.

He went up the stairs to his bedroom. Stripping off his clothes he showered, then stood in front of the magnifying mirror lathering his face prior to shaving.

The face looking back was still showing signs of the Afghan sun. His hair was dark with a hint of silver at the temple; he was five foot eleven inches tall and a lean twelve stone in weight; his eyes were dark green hazel.

His last living relative had died leaving the cottage and three hundred thousand pounds to him. He could barely remember his benefactor, the only brother of his mother, who had lived his entire life as a virtual recluse dying aged eighty nine in this same bedroom.

The sudden windfall had decided him to retire from the RAF, and take up residence in the old house. The last six months had flown as he, with some help from a local builder, had transformed the place. He looked about him with satisfaction. The building was stone built with walls two foot thick, a York stone roof and mullioned windows. The inside floor was flagged and there was an open wood burning fireplace. The ceiling was oak beamed, the walls rough plaster, now painted white. He had decided on some modernizations and installed oil fired central heating as well as a fully tiled bathroom with a large bath and a walk-in shower. It also had what must have been the only bidet in North Yorkshire.

Guy had always been a suit, shirt and tie man and although he was not adverse to casual clothes he somewhat regretted that standards had slipped, for instance in restaurants. For this reason Guy had a large fitted wardrobe installed, with drawers for shirts and a rack for shoes.

Outside, the yard had been covered in stone chippings, and the old barn cleaned out and repaired and was now used as a garage for his one extravagance – a black Porsche 911, his pride and joy.

There was also a couple of acres which in time could be used to grow vegetables, a pig pen and chicken coop, minus pigs and chickens.

He had visited antique shops in nearby Whitey and was now the proud owner of a large glass fronted display cabinet which would in time house his collection of Napoleonic figurines. He had also bought a leather Chesterfield settee and wing chair in green, the stone floor was covered by several Persian rugs which added colour as well as warmth.

He looked around with satisfaction; it was a man's room, some of the furniture had belonged to his uncle, the big kitchen table with the captains chairs, and a huge Welsh dresser, both quite valuable.

Attached to the kitchen was a utility room with fridge and washing machine. Another small room served as an office containing a small desk, filing cabinets and a computer.

He was aware that now his work to the cottage was complete he had to decide what to do about some kind of work. He was only thirty five, too young to retire and the improvements to the house had made a hole in the money left to him. He had a small pension from the RAF, plus money saved over the years, you don't spend much in Afghanistan, so there was no immediate need.

There was one other small room in the house, more of a large cupboard really, this was secreted to the rear of the fitted cupboard in the kitchen. Entry was by moving

Nemesis

a small lever which enabled the back panel to slide open. Inside was a rack holding two double barrelled shotguns and a 22 rifle. These had belonged to his uncle who had never bothered to ask the police for a licence. There was also a Luger pistol in a case, this his uncle had picked up when as a young tank commander he had landed on D Day. Ammunition for all the weapons was neatly stored on a shelf.

Guy did intend to make the guns legal, except the Luger, that would have to remain a secret. Guy glanced at his watch, an Omega Sea master, 13.00, must think about lunch.

Cooking was one thing that Guy was determined to master. He had bought several cook books and he was going through them page by page. Suddenly there was a knock on the door. Post man I expect, he thought as he made his way to open it.

Not the post man but his old batman Lac Cox.

"Well, of all the people to knock on my door."

"Sorry to bother you sir, but I was in the area and I thought …"

"No bother at all Cox, it's good to see you, the last time you were on a stretcher having just walked into an IED."

"Yes sir, a long time in dock, I lost my right leg below the knee."

"Yes, I heard about that. How is it now?"

"Well to be honest, can hardly tell because the knee joint was OK. They do some wonderful things with prosthetic limbs these days."

"So apart from that, I know you were married, how is your wife?"

"Divorce will be through any time, I found her in bed with the bloke from next door when I went home."

"Jesus I am sorry. Where are you living?"

"With my sister at the moment but she doesn't have room really so I will have to find somewhere."

"And what about a job?"

"Nothing at the moment but I have my disability and a bit saved up, I will be OK.

"Look, it's good to see you, stay and have some lunch and we will talk about old times."

"Well if you're sure sir. I don't want to be a nuisance."

"Don't be silly, it's really good to see you, you're my very first visitor."

They talked long into the afternoon and it was getting dark.

"Where are you staying tonight?"

"I'll find a pub or something sir, don't worry."

"Tell you what Cox, spend the night here, I have plenty of room and I will be glad of some company."

So after a meal of steak and chips they relaxed before the fire and drank a fine brandy.

*

Guy had been quiet for some time and was deep in thought.

"I have been thinking Cox, and please tell me if it

Nemesis

does not appeal to you. I live alone and shortly I will have to find work of some kind. How would it be if you worked for me? We could convert the barn's upper floor into a self-contained flat, and in time we could get some chickens and even pigs, the garden could be used to grow vegetables, and you could do your old job of looking after me. Whatever work I finally get will almost certainly mean me being away for weeks at a time, and I would be glad to have someone looking after the place. We have shotguns and you could go on the moor and shoot for the pot. We could be self sufficient. The only thing is wages, I could not afford much, but you would have free accommodation and food, and I will buy a secondhand four wheeler. I need one come winter anyway, what do you say?"

"I say *yes please* sir, to be honest I was hoping you might suggest something like that, it's more than I could ever wish for."

2

Next day after breakfast Guy and Cox sat in the kitchen drinking coffee and making plans for the next week.

"I have been asked to spend the weekend at the Lodge," said Guy. "Marcia is riding a point to point on Saturday, and her father has organized a rough shoot at the adjoining farm on Sunday. So would you lay out my dinner suit, my wax jacket and cords for the shoot, and my cap? I will travel down in a sports jacket, cavalry twill trousers and brown brogues, they will do for day wear as well."

"Very good sir. Will you take a gun?"

"No, I think it best that I borrow one for the day, but remember to pack my Hunters. It will be muddy. Now the next thing, you still have your hire car yes? OK, then on Tuesday we will go into Whitby, you can take the car back then we will look for a four wheeler, it will be best to have one before the bad weather. You can be thinking of what to do regarding the flat above the garage. We can get the ball rolling and see the builder at the same time we return your car."

"Yes sir, I have got all that. What time will you set off on Friday?"

"After breakfast I think about 9.30."

"Right. I'll prepare breakfast and give you a call about

Nemesis

8am, if that's all right."

Guy was more and more pleased about the fact that he now had Cox working for him, it was good for them both.

"By the way sir, I was wondering if you had any objection to dogs.?"

"No, but I would rather not have them in the house, what exactly do you have in mind?"

"Well, I know someone with a litter of pups, cross Labrador and Springer Spaniel, I could train them to fetch birds and pick up game, they would also be useful to keep any fox away from chickens when we get some."

"Good idea, do you have any idea how to go about training gun dogs because I haven't?"

"When I was a boy we had a small holding in Thirsk, I was used to dogs, chickens and even pigs, so yes sir I can train them, no bother."

"Right, that's settled then, what do you think, two seems about right?"

"Yes sir they could live outside in summer, I will knock up a couple of kennels. In the winter they would be OK in the barn, I will get on with it then."

*

Things seemed to be progressing nicely, but Guy had still not decided what he would do regarding a job.

Friday morning at 8.am on the dot a discreet knock on the bedroom door:

"Good morning sir, I have brought your tea, breakfast

in one hour."

Just like old times thought Guy, it had always been Cox's habit to wake him with hot tea.

He shaved and showered and went downstairs wearing his bath robe, don't want to mess my shirt with egg yolk he thought.

The TV, was on and the news was still about the terrorist attacks in Europe.

"What can be done to stop these bastards?" said Guy.

"Well, we did our best sir and look what happened. We lost some good lads out there. The buggers don't even fight like men face to face."

"Right then I'm off, I'll see you Monday about lunch time I would think."

3

Guy drove out of the yard taking care not to flick the stone chippings up; he was looking forward to the drive. It had been ages since he had last driven the car.

It was his favourite way of relaxing, some people found driving made them tense and irritable but he never had. He often completed a journey almost without realizing he was driving. He called it his 'automatic pilot', the good thing was he could drive for hours without feeling tired.

Traffic was light and he made good time, always with one eye in the mirror looking for police. One drawback with the 911, was the fact you could be doing a hundred before realizing it.

He arrived at the Lodge and pulled up outside the front entrance. Walters the butler was outside in a flash. He must get information that guests were due from a lookout in the village Guy thought.

"Mr Guy, welcome, we have not had the pleasure of your good self for months. Leave your luggage beside the car sir and I will see it's taken to your usual room. Sir James and Lady Pamela are in the library, I will inform them of your arrival."

Guy walked towards the library to be greeted by Jasper the old Airedale who must be at least twelve years old.

Nemesis

"Hello Jasper," said Guy, stroking his woolly head. "How are you boy?"

Lady Pamela came to meet him and lifted her face to be kissed.

"Hello Guy, how lovely to see you."

I understand you are now a man of property, is all the building work completed.?

"More or less still some fine tuning but yes we are nearly there."

"Come in and say hello to Sir James, he has been so looking forward to your visit, Marcia is out riding, she was on the horse about five minutes after arriving."

Sir James stood as Guy entered the room.

"Good to see you my boy how does it feel to be a civilian then?"

"Took some getting used to at first Sir, but we were so busy getting the place up to scratch I had no time to think.

You remember my batman Cox? Well he arrived out of the blue and to cut a long story short I have employed him to help about the place."

"Well done my boy, that's what we used to do in my day, you may not realize it but Walters used to be my batman. It's the least we can do to reward them for caring for us."

"Marcia will be back soon," said Lady Pam.

"We will have a cold lunch if that's alright and then this afternoon she wants to walk the course for tomorrows point to point."

– 13 –

Nemesis

"That's a good idea, I'll see if she wants company, I could do with some exercise after the long drive" said Guy.

The sound of hooves could be heard from the stable yard and the door flew open seconds later and Marcia flung herself into his arms.

"God I have missed you," she said kissing him on his mouth.

"Hey, steady on young lady" said Guy. "You know what I am like when I see you in jodhpurs and boots, I will forget where I am and ravish you here and now."

"The way I feel I wouldn't put much of a fight, but let's wait for later."

"About that," Guy said. "Do you think your parents know you creep down to my room after we are all supposed to be asleep?"

"Of course they do silly, but they respect the fact it's done discreetly rather than the modern way of just taking it for granted."

*

Lunch was served in the dining room, ham, cheese, pork pies, and fresh bread, complemented by a chilled bottle of Chardonnay.

"We will take our coffee in the library Walters" said Lady Pam, "and then you two can inspect the course."

"I worry you know when you take part in point to points" said Lady Pam.

"I know your an excellent rider but it's so dangerous,

please promise me you will be careful."

"Take the Range Rover Guy" said Sir James, "it's muddy across the meadow and I don't think your motor was designed for it."

So kitted up in wax Burberry and hunters they strolled around the course, Marcia making notes on a pad of the more difficult sections.

Guy was telling her about the cottage and the work he had done since taking over.

She was delighted to hear about employing Cox who she had met on many occasions.

"I think it's a great idea, she said, "from the sound of it there is much to do if as you say your thinking of pigs, and chickens.

"By the way Guy, I did not say anything before but Robert is due down sometime today and I know he wants a quiet word with you."

4

Robert was Marcia's older brother by some ten years, Guy knew he worked for the government but it was always a mystery exactly which department

He knew that before taking the job he had been a Major in the marines, and that for part of his service he had been attached to the SBS, Special Boat Squadron.

"What does he want do you think?"

"If I was guessing I would say its about a job," said Marcia.

"When do you think you might be able to come up and see the old place?" said Guy.

"The cottage is finished and I would like you to give it the once over, I have plans to convert the barn into a flat for Cox but I don't think it will take long, most of it is there already."

"Well I'm very busy but I dare say I could get away next month for a week or so."

"Good that's a date then. Come up by train and I'll meet you at the station."

"Let's go back home now, I am dying for a bath, and bet you are too. We will be dressing for dinner you have brought your suit?"

"Yes I know the form by now. It's nice to take the trouble. It's a dying practise now but it makes it more of an occasion."

Guy found his dress suit laid out on his return, a subtle reminder should he have forgotten.

He laid in the huge old iron bath and turned on the tap with his foot, more hot water flowed until he could bear it no longer,but he could feel the tension easing from his body.

He made his way down to join the others for pre dinner drinks, Marcia stood in front of him and said "I see your still having trouble with your tie, here let me. There that's better."

Guy noticed Robert had arrived and he came up and shook hands,

"Nice to see you Guy, look I've had a word with sis, and asked if I could have ten minutes with you before dinner. Pa says we can use his office.

Robert sat at the desk, Guy took a chair opposite,

"There is someone I would like you to see. Could you come to London next week and I will arrange a meeting? Sorry to be so mysterious but it is better you see him face to face. What I can tell you is that it concerns a job, you may not be interested in which case you can go back home.

If on the other hand you are interested, we would want you to stay down there for about three days, either way we will pay all expenses for travel and hotels."

"Well Robert, it all sounds very exciting. The only thing is Marcia has arranged a visit to my place in Yorkshire starting on the tenth of next month, would it interfere with that?"

"Not in the least Guy, we will be pleased to work around any plans you may have."

"Well in that case, *yes*. Would Thursday of next week be good for you?"

"Thursday will be fine, come by train and I will arrange a meeting for 1pm, we will take you to lunch and then get down to business."

"It would be best if you wear a suit, I know you have an excellent wardrobe, pack for a few days."

They joined the other guests in the library, the talk with Robert had taken no more than ten minutes.

Marcia raised an eyebrow but Guy shook his head and said "Asked me to attend a meeting next week in London, that's all I know."

5

Dinner was a pleasant affair, soup, a fish course, and saddle of lamb, and bread and butter pudding to finish.

Afterwards they adjourned to the library for a game of cards for those who wanted, or simply sat and talked sipping a fine old brandy.

Marcia excused herself at eleven saying she had a big day coming up, and a big night before that young lady thought Guy.

Guy lay in the large old canopied bed and listened to the ticking of the wall clock. He lifted his wrist to glance at the illuminated face of the Omega Sea master – 1.30 – perhaps she had being serious about the early night.

Silently the bedroom door opened and Marcia stood there, her dressing gown slipped from her shoulders and Guy marvelled at the slim gym toned figure, the small firm breasts and the dark triangle at the base of her stomach.

He lifted the covers and she slid in beside him

"I've longed for this moment" she said, her hands were stroking his chest moving slowly to the right shoulder to touch the bullet scar.

She kissed his shoulder gently,

"Does it give you any pain darling?"

Nemesis

"No the only thing that hurts at the moment is lower down."

"Don't worry Marcia will take away the pain" she said as her hand moved slowly down his body.

She took him in her hand.

"My you are a big boy" she said running her fingers up and down until he could stand it no longer.

He rolled her on his back and kissed her breasts taking each nipple in turn until they were like pebbles.

His hand moved its way towards that secret place brushing his fingers through the pubic hair until he found the little button that gave her such pleasure.

She was already wet and ready. Her fingers closed over his penis as she guided him into her breathing a sigh of contentment.

Their lovemaking was fast and both climaxed within a few seconds,

"Don't worry darling" she said. "The second and third times will take longer."

She took over control stroking him into another erection within minutes.

"I will get some practise for tomorrow" she said as she mounted him guiding him into her again.

She sat astride back straight rocking forwards and backwards driving him slowly mad afterwards they lay in each others arms quiet and spent, as dawn broke Marcia rose, put on her dressing gown and quietly let herself out.

*

Nemesis

Breakfast was served in the dining room. Help yourself from tureens, bacon scrambled eggs, kippers orange juice, and coffee

Marcia was dressed for the point to point which would start at two pm, plenty to do before that.

There was a country show with stalls selling clothing and all the gear for riding and shooting, there was a dog show, horse jumping as well as Punch and Judy for the children.

The weather was good and large crowds expected, the beer tent and hot dog stalls were doing brisk business.

Guy was deep in thought about the coming trip to London and why it was so secret.

He knew Robert worked for some government department and it had never been clear what he did exactly. Could it be something to do with security.

The afternoon passed quickly, Marcia acquitted herself well in the event and finished well up the order. Then it was back to the house, bath and change once again for dinner, with another pleasant evening in prospect.

The bedroom gymnastics went even better than the previous night with one or two variations introduced to the satisfaction of both.

Sunday morning dawned, a fine day in prospect, Guy borrowed a gun and the three men walked through the field about fifty yards apart.

The beaters dogs flushed a couple of hares and several rabbits which would make cook happy, then home for lunch.

All too soon it was time to go. Guy thanked Sir James and Lady Pam for an enjoyable weekend and they promised to come to Yorkshire very soon to look over his new home.

The parting from Marcia was worse and Guy knew he would miss her, but she had her career which she loved and neither were ready for marriage yet.

"See you Thursday" said Robert

"Yes looking forward."

Just wish I knew more about it thought Guy.

The trip home was uneventful and Guy pulled into the yard about 7pm, Cox had been busy and had prepared a meal knowing Guy would be famished.

"I'll just have time for a quick shower before we eat" said Guy.

*

"Any news regarding the building work?" asked Guy as they ate dinner.

"Well sir it's a matter for you, but I have measured the floor space and we have 150 square metres, we have enough room to really go to town,

On the ground floor I thought a workshop and more storage but that still leaves enough room for a gym, we could even build a sauna with the left over timber.

"That's a great idea Cox. Put a weights machine in and a sit up bench. Give us something to do on a winters night."

"Do you need me for anything tonight sir? If not, I'll nip down to the pub."

"You do, I'll listen to music and have an early night."

He had not slept much at the weekend, Marcia had seen to that.

I'll need a gym he thought if she keeps this pace up.

6

The next day there was much to do, first thing was return the hire car. Cox drove and Guy followed in the Porsche.

"Right let's look at some four wheel drive vehicles."

The local dealer had a good selection as most people in the area owned one.

They looked at several and Guy found himself drawn to a Daihatsu diesel. It was second hand but low mileage and a good thing was it had a tow bar.

They also decided on a trailer, this would be used to carry timber and logs.

So that was it, deal done a motor and trailer and a full tank of fuel thrown in.

"Right" said Guy, "Follow me to the demolition yard I remember seeing some oak floorboards from a school which they had just finished working on."

They were still there and after talking to the owner of the yard they bought enough to cover the upper floor of the barn. Guy paid another twenty pounds for them to be put through a skimming machine. This would ensure a good surface.

The demo man agreed to carry out the work and would deliver next week.

"Good" said Guy. "Follow me again."

Next stop was to the architect who had designed the

alterations to the cottage.

"Call and see us on Wednesday. I want some plans drawing up for the top floor of the barn converting to living accommodation,"

Next stop was the local builder who previously had carried out some work. He had always proved reliable and his work first class.

Guy explained what he had in mind.

"The building is sound, stone walls and the same York stone roof as in the cottage. The first thing I want the pest control man to give the place a good clean, I want all timber treated for infestation. You must realize it has been used as a barn for two hundred years. I will give you the plans when I have them but we will need a new staircase, windows at second storey level, oil fired central heating, bathrooms, bedrooms and so on.

We have bought all the flooring and the rest can be constructed of stoothing walls and plaster board. You know the form, plans may change as we go on but that's the general idea. The thing is though, I want it done quickly, once you start you will have to keep at it until completion. Is that something you can manage? Now is the time to say yes or no."

"No problem, I can organize all trades to save you the bother, act as it were as clerk of works, if that suits you."

"That's exactly what I want, you shall have the plans as soon as they are drawn up, we also need planning permission but I don't think that's a problem."

Nemesis

*

"You certainly know how to get things done sir, I can't believe how quickly you organized that lot it would take me weeks."

"Right Cox, you are going to be alone for the next few days. On Thursday I am going to London. Will you lay out my navy suit, shirts and ties etc.? I will travel in the suit and take some casual gear as well, enough for at least three or four days. To be honest I am a little in the dark as to what I do take. So pack some jeans too. Are you OK with everything, money for instance?"

"Yes sir, no problem. While you're away I'll organize some logs for the winter. I was talking to a farmer in the pub and he was saying that a couple of trees had blown down last year. We have a deal that I take what I want as long as I cut some for him at the same time. Now we have the trailer and the chain saw I will get enough to last us the year."

On the Wednesday the architect arrived and they went through what would be needed.

"I think two bedrooms, a bathroom, kitchen and lounge, with store and utility rooms."

"We might as well use all the space we can, I was saying to the builder the stairs are looking a bit dodgy so we'll have new ones I'll leave it with you. We can always fine tune later."

7

Thursday morning, Guy was on his way to the station in the Daihatsu with Cox driving.

"I have no idea how long I'll be away but as soon as I know I'll tell you" said Guy.

The journey down was boring but Guy consoled himself by thinking I'll soon know what this is all about. He took a taxi from Kings Cross to the address he had been given, this turned out to be a street to the rear of horse guards, right in the centre of power thought Guy.

A big shiny black door with a number, no brass plate or any indication what lay behind.

He opened the door and found a commissionaire seated at a desk, "Good morning Sir may I help you?"

"Good morning to you, my name is Bennett I have an appointment at one pm."

The commissionaire consulted a list and said:

"Yes sir, you are expected. Please take a seat, someone will be with you shortly."

Guy had hardly sat down when Robert appeared.

"Hello Guy, come with me you can leave your case here."

He followed Robert through the first door to be confronted by another. This one had a glass fronted pad at the side.

Nemesis

Robert placed his hand palm down on the pad and the door swung open. Down a short passage to yet another door, again Robert placed his hand on the pad and again the door opened.

They were now in a large beautifully furnished room, oil paintings hung from the walls expensive carpets littered the floor, and there were several highly polished doors leading off.

Robert stopped by one door and opened it, Guy followed him into a large room with a huge desk beneath the French window. Again the furnishing was expensive and very old, large leather settees and chairs lined the walls and a chandelier hung from the ceiling probably costing more that Guy's cottage.

A small man rose from behind the desk and approached with hand outstretched. He wore a beautifully cut suit which screamed Seville Row.

"How do you do. Allow me to introduce myself, I am Sir Ronald Swift."

Guy shook his hand surprised to feel the strength of his grip. They sat together at a small table.

"Robert, ask Fiona to bring tea while we have a chat with Guy. Now then, I'll assume you know nothing of our organization Guy."

"Absolutely sir" replied Guy. Robert was cryptic to say the least.

"Well, we know all about you, we have your service record of course but apart from that we prepared a dossier on more or less your entire life."

"And why would you, sir, if I may ask?"

"Because in our line of work we have to be sure that we have the right man even before we have one of our little chats. For instance, we know that you developed martial arts skills not taught in any gym. The only people who practise this way of fighting are the Israelis and more important, their secret service *Mossed*. It has no name but one objective – to kill using any part of the body. It is not an Olympic event and few know of its existence. You, on the other hand, went out of your way to find someone to teach you ... we like that. We know from your service record that you are a crack pistol shot, and that you speak five languages fluently."

The tea had arrived and Sir Ronald paused until the girl had left the room.

"How do you take it, milk and sugar?"

"Milk only sir" said Guy. "You make me sound like James Bond."

"Funny you should say that," said Sir Ronald. "Perhaps we should explain what this is all about. Robert first brought you to my attention whilst you were a serving officer but it could go no further. Now you are ... shall we say *unemployed* ... we felt the time was right to approach you. Let me ask, have you being following the news of the terrorist attack in Brussels?"

"Yes, as a matter of fact I have" said Guy.

"Well," continued Sir Ronald, "you may be surprised to hear that the brains behind the attack was arrested more or less immediately afterwards."

Nemesis

"That's good, I'm pleased."

"Yes, but you won't be too pleased to hear that he was released after screaming for a lawyer to which he was entitled, or so he said.

"Now there is no doubt that he is guilty, the Belgium secret service have being following him for months but they can't make a case that would satisfy the morons who quote civil liberties.

Our little department was set up in secret, even the PM knows nothing of it, *our aim is justice and our methods are terminal.*"

"I don't know what to say" said Guy. "One hears about this sort of thing but dismiss it as pure fiction."

"The thing is Guy are you for or against the taking of life without benefit of trial and jury? If you decide that it's wrong there's no ill feeling. All we would ask is that you never mention this interview which never took place."

"When I was in the RAF, we would go on patrol, and I have seen young men of nineteen killed or maimed by LEDs. One of the reasons I left was because nothing was done about it. We still had to play the hearts and minds game even though we knew beyond a doubt that the bastard who rigged up the trap was standing in front of me. Does *that* answer your question sir? If you want me, I am in."

"*Splendid.* Robert was sure that would be your answer. We will go and have some lunch at my club and afterwards go into more detail."

Nemesis

"How are you fixed for time Guy?" said Robert. "We have made a tentative booking for two weeks at the Green Park Hotel in Half Moon street. This will give us all the time we need to put you in the picture."

"No problem, I told Cox I expected to be away for some time and I've brought enough gear to last."

After a convivial lunch at Sir Ronald's club they headed back to headquarters.

"I feel we have done enough for one day Guy. The best thing would to get you settled and then meet again at say 9.30."

*

A taxi dropped Guy at the hotel which is situated about one mile from Piccadilly Circus in one direction, and Bond Street in the other.

After unpacking, Guy decided on a stroll before dinner. It had been years since he had spent any time in the capital and he did not think there would be much time for sightseeing in the next few weeks. He walked along Regent Street, down Seville Row and was making his way back to the hotel and looking in the brightly lit windows of Bond Street.

As he turned the corner of the street that led to *Trumpets*, the famous barbers shop that boasted among its many distinguished patrons the Prince of Wales, he became aware of footsteps behind.

Suddenly there was a hand on his shoulder and on turning around was confronted by four black youths.

Nemesis

The one at the front held up a knife and said

"Give us your phone, cash and watch whitey."

"How do you want to play this?" said Guy. "You can walk away, or I can put the four of you in intensive care, your choice."

A look of astonishment appeared on the face of the leader: this is not what happens, people just hand over their stuff and if they're lucky we don't hurt them.

One of the gang had manoeuvred himself to Guy's rear, he can be first.

Guy's right elbow slammed into the guy's gut followed by the edge of his hand catching him just under the nose. This was a killer blow if delivered with full force – in this case it was not.

The lad went down out of the fight, Guy's right foot stamped on knife man right knee with an ominous crack. Two left he whirled round grabbing the one to his left by his collar and bringing his head down butted him on the nose.

One left, no he was running as fast as his legs would carry him, Guy bent down arranged the left leg of knife man so that it was on the road, his body on the pavement.

When he was satisfied with the position he lifted his foot above the knee and then brought it down with all the power of his body.

The man let out a blood curdling scream, at best he would walk with a limp for the reminder of his life.

Guy paused only to retrieve the switch blade knife

from the pavement and then he continued to walk to the hotel – the whole thing had taken three minutes.

It's a good job I'm in a good mood he thought or I would have really hurt them. Anyway they would not be out mugging for a considerable time.

Back at the hotel he ate a light supper then turned in for an early night, he wondered what tomorrow would bring and after turning off the light was asleep in seconds.

8

Guy breakfasted early and dressed in a single breasted navy suit, white shirt and a red tie. His shoes were black slip-on tasselled loafers.

Might as well make a good impression he thought as he paid the taxi driver and walked to the black painted front door.

Robert was waiting in the foyer greeting Guy with a good morning. They followed the same route as the previous day but passed the door to Sir Ronald's office to enter one further along.

"This is my office" said Robert. "We are going to run through the programme for the next couple of weeks, and I will explain our modus operandi. The first thing we will do is take ten or so photographs of you all different, in some you will have a beard, others wigs of different colours, some with glasses etc.. These will then be used to make an assortment of passports all of different nationalities. All the real thing."

So they left the office and entered a studio on the second story, a technician was waiting camera at the ready.

"But first the make up artist" said Robert.

Guy sat in front of a mirror and an elderly man with long flowing hair entered the room.

Guy took one look and thought I bet he bats for the

other side, he was the epitome of an old queen.

"This gentleman" said Robert "was in another life an actor, what he doesn't know about make up is not worth knowing. In the next couple of weeks he will be your instructor in the art of disguise, for now he will give you five different faces."

The make up artist set to work.

"First new face a moustache, and goatee beard, and I think a pair of rimless spectacles, yes I think that's good."

Guy looked in the mirror and a complete stranger looked back. Photograph taken. That disguise was removed.

"Now I think I will change the colour of your eyes and pad your cheeks to give a fuller face."

Another photograph taken and yet another change of appearance magically produced, and so it went on all morning.

Finally they came to the last picture.

"I have made it as simple as I can, because you will have to do it yourself, don't worry you will be surprised how quickly you get the hang of it. It doesn't need to be anything elaborate, people don't really take any notice. Putting on a pair of glasses can change your looks. The problem is the passports, you must get used to the face in each one. I will make you practise until I am satisfied."

*

Nemesis

Back in Robert's office they sat drinking tea brought in by the same girl as before.

"What a morning, I'm exhausted" said Guy.

"Don't worry, we will have a quiet afternoon, I will just run through a few things. By the way Guy, three tough looking teenagers were found by the police last night, they tried to make out they had been attacked by a white man answering your description. The police don't believe a word, it turns out they all have form for mugging, but in this case it went badly wrong for them. They will be released from hospital in about three weeks, sadder and wiser I would think.

"Now some lunch, then I will give you an idea how we work."

After lunch, not quite as grand as yesterday's, Robert got down to the nuts and bolts of the job.

"The passports will be placed in boxes kept in the vaults of HSB banks in all the major city's in Europe. Also in these boxes will be cash in various currency a Clock pistol, an empty magazine next to it, and a box of 9mm, this will save the spring because you may not need that particular weapon for years. There will be a first aid kit, and the telephone number of a doctor, one of ours. There will also be a make up kit including everything you will need to change your appearance to whichever passport you intend to use. As well as the cash there will be credit cards – all valid – plus driving licences for most

European countries.

"You will be issued with a phone, this is a normal phone and will stand the test of examination by anyone, but if you press the on button six times quickly it will change into an encrypted phone giving complete security. This will include telephone numbers, addresses, and habits of any potential hit. There is also a signal transmitted by the phone which gives us your location at all times, this works even if the phone is turned off. You will be given a number which when produced at the banks will give you access to your box – we thought your service number would be best, as you never forget it.

So Guy, as soon as you persuade the make up man that you are able to change your looks you can go home, just lead your normal life we will be in touch if and when we need you.

One thing that is very important, we have not discussed a cover story. Each time you do, let us say … *a job*, £2,000 will be deposited in a Swiss bank of your choosing. This will be free of any tax. But Marcia and Cox, as well as anyone else who you know, will be curious as to what you do for a living. Your cover will be, you work as a consultant for a security firm, one of the many false flags we use, if anyone uses the telephone number on your business card the call will be answered by our switchboard. The operator will give the fictitious name of the company thereby conforming your cover. Your legend will include everything a normal employee would have, salary of £90,000 a year including private

Nemesis

health of course. All your expenses will be paid through this fictitious firm, and you will have an accountant, again one of ours who will take care of your tax etc.. So Guy, is there anything you want to ask me? If not you can start tomorrow getting used to the making up."

"No Robert, I'm sure I will think of something later but for now OK."

"Just one last thing, from now on you are *no longer Guy*. When you are here, your code name is *Nemesis*, defined in the dictionary as retribution or vengeance. Saturday tomorrow but no rest for the wicked, I want you to follow one of our operatives around London," said Robert. "He is aware of the fact and the object of the exercise is that he does not spot you, I know this is a difficult task in view of the fact that you have no training but let's just see how you do. Come in Sunday about ten and we will evaluate your performance."

*

Saturday: Guy picked up his target walking through Admiralty Arch. The man was wearing a dark overcoat and trilby hat.

Keeping a good hundred yards back Guy crossed over the road. I bet he ditches the hat and even the coat he thought, I must be ready for that.

The man paused in front of a shop window pretending to look at the display but Guy guessed he was using it as a mirror.

He continued on and went down in the tube

station,Guy following still about 50 yards behind. This is tricky thought Guy with various levels and platforms to choose from I will have to close the gap.

They both stood on the platform Guy well away to the other end, the train arrived and the man boarded as did Guy.

Just as the train doors began to close the man suddenly made a break for it and jumped out, Guy could only watch as his target walked out raising the finger in the air.

*

Sunday morning Robert sat behind his desk Guy in a chair opposite.

"Well, how do you think it went?"

"Not good to be honest, I fell for the doll trick in the tube, I should have considered him jumping off again."

"Tell you what, let's have him in and ask his opinion."

The man who had acted as a target came in and shook hands with Guy.

"Don't sell yourself short, you actually did well for someone who has had no special training in surveillance. I liked the way you crossed the road, it took me some time to find you again and *I* do this for a living. By the end of your time down here I am confident you will be able to follow most people without being spotted."

*

Nemesis

The next few weeks passed in a flash, Guy was amazed how soon he could change his appearance by the simple application of a wig, beard, or even a pair of spectacles.

His surveillance technique improved too, he was shown how to alter his appearance with a variety of hats and reversible coats and his instructors expressed their admiration at his willingness to improve.

Guy was called to what he referred to as headquarters on the Monday morning for a meeting with Sir Ronald, also present was Robert.

"Well Guy, you have more than proved your ability, all your instructors are extremely pleased with you as are Robert and myself. Go back home and carry on as normal, we will send for you in due course. There is no need to report here all information will be available on your device. You will organize your own travel arrangements, you have our complete confidence that any mission will be carried out in a professional manner."

9

Guy settled his hotel bill and called a taxi to Kings Cross. On the way he made a call to Cox and asked him to pick him up on Tuesday at the Post House Hotel in Leeds.

He had decided to make a detour in order to visit his tailor in Chapletown Leeds. Guy had used the same Jewish tailor for years. He was an old man now but still made a suit from start to finish sitting cross legged on the floor.

First port of call on arrival in Leeds was a taxi to the Post House Hotel in Bramhope. After checking in and dropping his bags he took another taxi to the old man's shop, he walked in and Mr Stankler appeared from the back room.

"Hello Mr Stankler. How are you today?"

"Mr Guy it's so long I thought you had found a man who made suits better than me."

They went through the same ritual every time he called.

"Well I did but you are much cheaper so I thought I would give you another chance."

The old man laughed and took the tape measure from around his neck. "What will it be this time?"

"I think a light grey worsted single breasted suit and a blue blazer."

Nemesis

"I know, leave plenty of room in the shoulder" the old tailor said. "The first time you ever came you said that to me, as though I would make it too tight."

Guy loved the old chap he must have had at least twenty garments made up for him over the years, and never a bad one.

The measuring over, the old boy insisted on a cup of coffee before Guy could leave.

"When can we do a fitting?" said the old man. "How about a week today?"

"Yes, I can manage that. I have some business in Leeds. I'll see you then."

Just for old times sake Guy caught a bus to the centre and walked round the city where he was born and lived until he had joined the RAF. How the place had changed, he felt like a stranger as he walked around the new shopping malls and pedestrian only areas. The market was still there though.

He recalled the times he had visited the place, the game row where pheasants and rabbits had hung from hooks, and the butchers row with its many shops all next to one another.

He walked along Boar Lane towards City Square, the statue of the Black Prince on horse back and the naked nymphs holding torches aloft.

They must have shocked some people in those far off days when men were lucky to see even their own wives in the nude.

Well, enough of this nostalgia, he flagged a cab and asked for the Post House, a meal and an early night I think. To be honest he was ready for one. The last three weeks had been hard work.

10

Guy slept until nine, went down for a leisurely breakfast, then packed and sat in the foyer reading the Daily Mail.

He expected Cox about eleven It would take about one and a half hours in the Daihatsu.

Cox walked through the door at exactly that time.

"Good morning sir, have you had a good trip?"

On the way home Cox brought him up to date on the latest events.

"The plans are back for you to see, I filled the wood shed with enough timber to see us through the winter, and when we get back I have arranged to pick up the two puppies. I have picked two out sir, one is black the other cream, both bitches, they have had their inoculations and are ready to start training. To be honest I can't wait, their parents are both gun dogs and they will take to it no bother."

"Well I can see you have been busy. I have got myself fixed up with a job which will take me away for days at a time so it's just as well that you came along when you did."

"Now, speaking of that I told you when you arrived we would sort out a wage later."

"Don't worry about that sir I am just pleased you wanted me I am not bothered about money."

"Well that's nice to hear Cox but you must be paid. Now I know more about my own future I can offer you two hundred a week, free accommodation and grub, and the free use of the motor, what do you say?"

"Too much really sir, I don't need any thing like that."

"Well that's what you're getting anyway so *shut up*."

"Very generous sir, I won't let you down."

"I know that you silly bugger. Let's not talk about it any more."

As soon as they arrived home Cox set off to pick up the pups, one hour later he came back with the dogs in a small cage in the back of the Jeep.

He let them out and they ran around the yard inspecting their new surroundings letting out small squeaks which later would become barks.

Guy fell in love with them at once,

"What shall we call them?" he said.

"Well sir, I thought *you* can have the honour of naming them what do you think?"

Guy thought for a moment and then said,

"The black one is *Whiskey*, the cream one *Soda*."

That decided Guy left Cox in charge to feed and arrange their sleeping arrangements.

Cox returned shortly,

"I made a small pen to keep them out of mischief inside the barn, and a large kennel with blankets. They will probably cry tonight but its amazing how soon pups settle down."

"It's a good job I won't hear them or they would

probably finish up in bed with me" said Guy."

"Don't worry sir, in a week they will be running the place, it's never too early to start training, at first it's playing finding things, and that develops into bringing object back to you."

11

They ate dinner then settled in front of the fire drinks in hand,

"I will explain about my new job" said Guy.

Following the story suggested to him by Robert he said, "I will show you my new business card" fishing it out of his wallet.

Sentinel Security and Protection.
London.
Tel. 02. 3678921.
GA. Bennett. Consultant.

"This means that there will be trips abroad from time to time, never more than a few days as a rule," said Guy. "You will have plenty to occupy you looking at those two puppies, plus of course supervising the new building. I've glanced through the proposed plans and they seem OK, do you have anything to add?"

"No sir, except to suggest we make the best possible use of the space upstairs, I was thinking more about storage than living space."

"I agree, you can never have too much storage room. I'll have a word with the architect. I will be going to Leeds again on Monday, I've shopping to do and a fitting with my tailor."

Nemesis

Before going upstairs to bed Guy opened the secret compartment at the rear of the cupboard and placed the switch blade knife he had taken from the mugger on the shelf. Even Cox was unaware of this small room, not that Guy mistrusted him. It was just a case of need to know.

The weekend was taken up doing the normal jobs one does when living in the wilds. The puppies had settled down and loved playing in the barn sniffing around and play fighting.

Cox had brought the floor boards into the barn to protect them from the weather. They were now a lovely shade of dark yellow having been put through the skimmer.

*

Monday came and Guy dressed in sports coat and slacks with a cashmere polo came downstairs, he took his Burberry black raincoat and threw it on the rear seat, it looked a bit like rain.

The journey to Leeds took about ninety minutes, he parked in the Merrion centre and made his way into the shops.

First stop was a shop that specialized in mirrors, he looked around and finally selected one that had a battery operated light and a magnified face. It also had a collapsible stand and came with a leather case, it was expensive but was exactly right.

Next stop was luggage.

Nemesis

He chose an aluminium roll on hard case bag small enough to take in the cabin, the last thing wanted was to wait at the carousel.

A pair of leather driving gloves were next on the list, black and tight fitting.

Think that's about all. No I'll buy a black cap one I can stick in my pocket to change my looks if following someone.

Back to the car and off to see Mr Stankler for my fitting, the old tailor was ready for him as he stood sticking pins in the material until he was satisfied.

"Your order will be ready by Friday Mr Guy, he said.

"OK, thanks. I'll call you if anything changes said Guy.

*

Back home he changed into jeans and a sweater and walked around taking everything in. He was pleased with the way it was falling into place.

Thank God I had the sense to employ Cox he thought, don't know what I would have done without him.

After a good dinner Guy sat and thought about Marcia's impending visit, as far as I can see we are ready to receive guests. The inside of the cottage looks nice, and I'm sure she will like the new bathroom, my biggest worry is that she will try and talk me into loads of ornaments – women like that sort of thing.

Today was Tuesday, Marcia had arranged her visit for Monday. Next, the telephone rang, it was the architect

Nemesis

to say that the plans had been passed and building could begin ASAP.

Guy rang the builder and asked him to start the work at once. It would not get in the way of Marcia's visit and the sooner Cox had his own place the better.

The telephone rang yet again, most unusual thought Guy, we go weeks without a call and then get two together.

This time it was Marcia.

"Sorry Guy, but I'm not going to make next week something has come up at work"

Marcia was a senior partner in a firm of sports management. Her job was to look after contracts and guest appearances for several sports men and women. Christian Scott Brown was a young British racing driver who had been strongly tipped to sign for Ferrari next season.

"We are having last minute problems over his contract, I will have to go to Italy and sort it out."

"How long will it take do you think?" said Guy.

"Lord knows, but then it's Wimbledon and I have promised to be there for Judy Simmons the American tennis player. Best thing is we reschedule for sometime in May. I know it's awful but I can't help it, the job comes first."

"OK, I understand, don't worry love we are up to our necks here so it may be a blessing in disguise. I'll be in touch and sort something out in a few days, take care and don't let those Italians pinch your bum."

Nemesis

Guy was disappointed but in a way it might be better later on when the building work was finished.

The workmen arrived next morning, Guy and the builder studied the drawings to decide the most effective way to work.

"Look I can't keep calling you the builder, what's your name?"

"It's John."

"OK, John. I'm Guy. Now how shall we start?"

"Well Guy the old staircase is still sound so I suggest we keep that in place for the time being, we will be carrying material to the second floor and it won't matter if some damage happens. First we will fit the central heating pipes and main electrics over the old ceiling joist, and them the reclaimed floor boards over the entire area. After that we will form the rooms in timber, that way you won't see any pipes leading to the radiators. Plaster board, second fix electrics, radiators and skirting and we are very nearly there. The last thing will be the new staircase and then it's just a case of decorating."

"I've been thinking" said Guy. "Do you think we have enough room for a guest bedroom and en suite?"

"Yes, I'm sure we have, the barn has more than enough space for a large bedroom whist still leaving enough for storage."

"Well" said Guy "you seem to know what your doing I'll leave it to you."

12

Guy **was sitting** in front of the fire, glass of red wine in hand when his special phone rang.

"Yes" he said. A voice on the other end said *"Go six"*, that he knew meant turn on the encrypted section of the phone.

The computer came to life.

> **Subject Mohammed Arak, (Terminate)**
> **Habits, takes coffee each morning in the main square Brussels around nine am.**
> **One or sometimes two guards definitely armed.**
> **Instigate ASAP.**

Guy went upstairs he opened the large fitted wardrobe he selected under clothing, shirts and tie and put those on the bed. A dark suit, black shoes and socks, these also were put on the bed.

How long? he thought, no more than three days. Max, two more likely.

He went downstairs to his office and booted up the computer. He found a Jet Two flight to Brussels from Leeds and Bradford Airport leaving at 2pm, the following day. He booked a single way ticket in case the job took longer than anticipated. Back upstairs he placed his passport, wallet and credit cards and some Euros along side the other items.

Cox, as it happened, had gone to the local pub again. He waited for his return and told him he would be going away for possibly two days. He then went to bed.

Normally Guy had no trouble sleeping but tonight his mind was racing as he went through the pros and cons.

The drive to Leeds gave him the chance to sort things out in his mind, he would examine the area around the square observing Arak and try to work out the best place to carry out the hit and more importantly escape afterwards.

*

Arriving in Brussels he cleared customs and took a taxi to the city centre, he found a nice looking hotel called *Hubert Grand Palace*, right on the main square. He registered and presented his passport and credit card.

"How many nights Sir?" asked the desk clerk.

"Three I think, but it might be more. Is that OK?"

"No problem Sir. Just let the desk know."

She gave him the key for room 3521.

"Have a nice stay Sir."

The room was what one would expect from a four star hotel, it looked directly on to the square and Guy was particularly pleased to note there was a safe in the wardrobe. He unpacked and placed his passport in the safe, he then took the lift to reception and walked through the swing door.

Nemesis

He stopped for a sandwich and coffee at a small bar and then made his way to the HSBC bank.

He asked the guard in the foyer the procedure for opening his box.

"One second sir I will get someone to help."

A young woman appeared and said

"I understand you want to examine your box Sir, what is your number?"

Guy recited the number and she said

"This way sir."

They entered a small room where hundreds of steel fronted doors, each with a lock, were round the walls. The young bank clerk took out a key, opened one of the small doors and withdrew a metal box about eighteen inches square and six inches in depth. This she placed on the table in front of Guy and said,

"When you are done just ring that bell."

She then walked out locking the door behind her.

Guy took the key given to him by Robert and opened the lid.

As expected there was an automatic Glock 19 semi automatic Pistol and magazine. He stuck the gun in the waistband of his slacks, the magazine in his pocket, he counted out seventeen 9mm. bullets and slipped them in a small plastic bag.

He then selected a passport from the several lying there. It was Belgium in the name of Lucas Peeters. The photograph inside was Guy wearing a goatee beard, moustache and rimless glasses.

Inside the passport was a credit card for HSBC, both items went into Guy's inside pocket.

He next picked up an envelope containing make up, various hair pieces and this too went into his pocket.

There was a bundle of American Dollars as well as some Euro notes. He stuck two fifties in his pocket leaving the dollars.

He locked the box and rang the bell. The clerk appeared at once and asked if everything was OK.

"Thank you, yes" said Guy as the box was returned to its place.

*

Guy walked round the square and found a street market in progress He bought a black anorak, a pair of jeans and some soft soled shoes. The next stall sold luggage, he bought a small holdall, all goods he paid for in cash. He took a seat on a bench and placed all the items in the bag. He then made his way back to the hotel.

Once in his room he removed his jacket, took the mirror he had bought in Leeds and set it up on the desk. He then took the Belgium passport and stood it in front of the mirror. Removing the false beard and moustache from the envelope he applied the adhesive to his chin and within fifteen minutes Lucas Peeters appeared.

He placed the gun, magazine and ammunition in the safe then he dressed in the jeans and anorak, put on the soft soled shoes, placed a few items of clothing into the bag to make it look full and took the lift down again.

Nemesis

He found a farmacia around the corner purchased a few cosmetic items, tooth brush, shaving foam, razor and comb, paid in cash then walked back to the hotel.

He went to reception and asked in French for a room for two nights, he surrendered his passport in the name of Lucas Peeters and was given the key for room 2432, the receptionist handed his passport back.

He walked to the lift got off at the second floor and opened the door to 2432.

Once inside he placed the cosmetics in the bathroom, locked the door and went up one floor in the lift.

He entered room 3521, removed the make up, placed the Belgium passport in the safe, changed into his own clothes again and was once again Guy Bennett.

Right thought Guy, I've done as much as I can today. I'll take a look at the square now and grab a bite to eat.

Guy sat at a table in the café where Arak went for his morning coffee. There were several tables out on the pavement, some with umbrellas.

It would depend on the weather where Arak decided to sit.

Between the café and the tables was an arched walkway stretching the length of the road with shops selling various items. There were several alleys leading off and after finishing his sandwich Guy examined each one.

He played the scenario over in his head, first there was the bodyguard to take into account, one or two that was the question.

He had no particular wish to kill the guards, just immobilize them but how? Would it be crowded? In some way he hoped it was. It is always easier to lose yourself among other people. As far as he could see the only problem was just after the hit, once he was away from the immediate area it would be a simple matter to get back to the hotel.

Now, let's see where he lives and the route he would take to the café.

The apartment where Arak lived was about ten minutes walk away, on route there were shops both sides of the street.

Guy had almost decided this was the best option rather than the square. There were several small streets leading off from the main road which would give him a chance to slip away. Would the bodyguard walk alongside Arak or a couple of yards to his rear? That's what I would do, he thought, of course if there were two guards they could do both!

Guy had decided that he would carry out the hit the day after next. He would by then know the method of protection exactly.

There was nothing else to do so he acted like any other tourist and enjoyed the city. Brussels is beautiful with some fine buildings and Guy relaxed for the first time in days.

*

Nemesis

Guy set his alarm for seven am. He showered and shaved and took the lift down to restaurant, he stood at the rostrum waiting to be shown to a table.

"Room 3521", he told the girl. He was shown to a small table and helped himself to bacon, scrambled eggs, and sausage. The waitress came around with fresh coffee and after two cups Guy left to go back to his room.

Once there he changed into Lucas Peeters again, he walked down one floor to room 2432, pulling on the soft leather gloves he had bought he opened the door.

He went into the bathroom and ran the shower for a few seconds, making sure his towel was damp, he then threw the covers from the bed and rolled about with his head on the pillow, then he filled a glass with water and left it next to the bed.

Taking the lift he went to the restaurant in his guise as Lucas Peeters and gave his room number 2432, to the girl, he was shown to a table and helped himself to breakfast.

He left the restaurant and took the lift to the third floor, where he put on the anorak and jeans and left the hotel.

*

After making his way to Arak's apartment he sat at a small snack bar and read a French newspaper keeping his eyes on the door.

At nine am the door opened and Arak came out

followed by one bodyguard. As Guy had thought the guard positioned himself about two yards to Arak's rear as they made their way to the square. Guy noticed that the bodyguard seemed alert, his head turning one way and another. He also noticed that his right hand was thrust into his coat pocket presumably holding a gun.

Guy followed at a discreet distance as they arrived at the café and decided to take one of the outside tables.

Guy went inside and sat where he could keep an eye on them. There was no conversation between Arak and the guard who continued to examine each person who came close.

One thing bothered Guy, he had thought to spare the life of the bodyguard but his devotion to his job was his own undoing. He could think of no way other than to kill him.

Guy had decided that the hit would take place the next day and with that in mind he booked a one way ticket to Leeds Bradford, Jet 2 leaving at 4pm. His plan was to carry out the hit in the disguise of Lucas Peeters. It was likely that the police would visit all hotels to check on recent visitors. It would be realized that Peeters had left the hotel without checking out, he had paid in advance but even so the police might be suspicious.

On checking the room it would be not what they found but what they *did not find* that would cause them to put out a search for him. They would not find a single fingerprint other than the maid's, and that Guy hoped would send them off on a wild goose chase.

Nemesis

Right, thought Guy, this is the day, he acted out the same scenario as before going down for breakfast making sure the room number was recorded.

Back in his room he became Lucas Peeters again, going down to room 2432 and clearing everything out after first putting on his gloves.

He went through the same ritual with the shower and towels, it was important to his plan that it looked as though Peeters had used the room. Before leaving for the last time he made sure that nothing had been left. He then walked up the steps to the third floor.

Entering room 3521 he dropped the bag containing the shaving gear and comb, he then hung the *"Do not disturb"* sign before going down to breakfast.

Again he made sure that room 2432 was recorded, afterwards he went upstairs to room 3521, he opened the safe and removed the gun.

He carefully loaded the magazine, and after first checking the mechanism snapped it into the Glock and pulled the slide. The gun was now hot, he slipped it in his rear waistband. Taking the lift to the ground floor he waited whilst the girl on the desk was busy with a new arrival and then walked out.

He sat at the same café opposite Mohammed Arak's apartment, ordered a coffee and opened his French newspaper. *Please let there be only one bodyguard* he prayed, the adrenaline was coursing through his veins and he tried to breathe deeply in an effort to control it.

Finally the door of the apartment opened, the bodyguard looked carefully up and down the street and then nodded his head to indicate that all was well.

Arak came out and down the steps to the street. As before the guard took up position about three yards to the rear.

Guy had made his move just as the bodyguard had been making sure there was no threat. He walked towards the square ducking into the first alleyway on the right, a quick check to make sure no one was in the street before removing the pistol.

Holding the gun by his side pointing at the ground he stood his back to the wall.

He heard the footsteps as Arak approached and the second he passed the alleyway Guy exploded from cover.

The bodyguard's reactions were good, his hand pulling his gun even though the surprise gave him little chance.

Guy's left hand connected to the left side of his neck in a vicious chop, Guy did not even bother to look he knew the blow was good and that it would incapacitate for a couple of minutes.

That was all the time needed to fire two rounds of nine millimetre into Arak's head.

Guy was already running down the alleyway until he approached an intersection he slowed down to a walk – nothing draws attention more than a running man.

Within ten minutes he was outside his hotel, a quick look through the revolving door showed about fifteen

Nemesis

people with luggage crowding around the reception desk.

He walked in using the stairs to the third floor. The do not disturb label was still on the door of room 3521, He entered and quickly removed the false beard,moustache and spectacles putting them in a paper bag.

He took out the passport in the name of Peeters and ripped it into small sections before putting in another paper bag.

The Glock he broke down to four components, those and the magazine he placed in his raincoat pocket.

The anorak,jeans and shoes along with the razor shaving cream and comb he put in the small hold all.

Lucas Peeters ceased to exist, there was no trace whatsoever. It was doubtful if any of the staff would even remember him.

Guy now took a long shower, shaved and washed his hair. He dressed in his suit and tie, checked he had left nothing then placed the small hold all inside his roll on case.

It was unlikely that it would be noticed that he had only one bag when registering, but why take the chance?

He left the room door wide open and took the lift downstairs to reception.

He paid his bill, thanked them for a pleasant stay and walked out, he could hear police sirens in the distance.

As he walked he passed waste bins, at each one he dropped sections of the passport, coming to a skip he dropped one bit of the gun, he would continue to get rid of it a piece at a time.

He passed a doorway in which a young man was asleep, he opened his roll on bag, took the hold all out and placed it by his side, he did not wake up but when he did he would find a new outfit.

A few days before whilst walking around Guy had seen a notice advertising a sale of Napoleonic memorabilia. That will pass the time before my flight he thought.

He found the exhibition on the ground floor of a hotel, what better place he thought, after all Belgium was the country the battle took place.

He looked around the display of weapons, there were swords, pistols and he was pleased to see figurines of French soldiers beautifully crafted and correct in all details. He could have spent all day but he was aware that he had to be two hours early for his flight. He could not resist, however, and purchased two cavalry sabres to hang on his wall and two figurines one of a Polish Lancer the other an Old Guard soldier at the present arms position. He paid and asked that they be delivered to the address in Yorkshire.

Not only had he acquired something for his collection, he had also provided a genuine reason for his trip should anyone ask.

A taxi dropped him at the airport, he booked in and made his way through security. He stopped in a café and ordered a sandwich and coffee.

Looking back over the day's events he was fairly confident that he had covered himself well, settling down he

Nemesis

unfolded the Daily Mail and waited for his flight to be called.

As expected the police did routine visits to hotels looking for anything unusual, two plain clothes officers visited the Hotel Hubert Grand Palace.

"Anything out of the ordinary?" they asked at reception.

"No, well maybe" said the clerk.

"What do you mean?" they asked.

"Well it's nothing really, but one guest failed to check out, it does happen sometimes if there are a lot of people at the desk and they can't be bothered to wait. He had paid his bill in advance, so perhaps it did not really matter."

"What nationality was he?"

"Belgian and he stayed two days."

"Well it's probably nothing but we might as well take a look at his room."

The maid let them in in with her pass key.

They looked around, the room had been made up for the next visitor and fresh towels were in the bathroom, clean sheets on the bed.

"Tell you what" said one policeman to the other, "we have nothing else so why don't we get fingerprints to have a look?"

Fingerprint technicians arrived and put powder in certain places, they then called the two cops back.

"Well we have either the most conscientious maid in

the world, or this person who stayed here wore gloves the entire time."

That was reason enough for further investigation.

The facts finally arrived on the desk of Chief Inspector Monet, Belgium Security.

He was the officer who had originally brought Arak in for questioning, and who had released him after his lawyer had read the riot act. Monet knew beyond a doubt that Arak was guilty, and frankly didn't give a shit that he was now in the morgue. Investigation had shown the Belgium passport to be genuine, but the address given was false and no one had heard of Lucas Peeters.

This has the hallmarks of being either CIA, MI6 or MOSSAD thought Monet, and good luck to whoever it was. He was not going to break his neck trying to find out.

*

The flight to the UK was uneventful, Guy cleared customs and picked the car up from the long stay park.

He pulled into the yard at eight o'clock, put the car in the garage and made his way inside.

"Good to see you sir, good trip?"

"Yes thank you Cox any news?"

"Works going well with the barn, the dogs are in everyone's way, but that's about it. I've made a pie sir, I thought you would be hungry when you arrived. I'll start getting it ready whilst you unwind."

"What would I do without you Cox? I'll have a quick

shower and be down in a tick."

After a decent meal and a few glasses of red wine Guy retired to his office.

He took out his special phone and opened the secret communication feature which allowed him complete security to pass any message without fear.

TOP SECRET. OPERATION COMPLETE (ARAKI) TERMINATED.
LUCAS PEETERS PASSPORT COMPROMISED. NEW LEGEND REQUIRED.
ITEMS TO BE RENEWED. GLOCK PISTOL AND MAG,
DISGUISE ENVELOPE.
100, EURO.
MESSAGE ENDS.
NEMESIS.

Guy hit the *send* button, turned off the light and retired to bed.

13

After a good breakfast Guy changed into jeans and a leather jacket and walked to the barn.

The builders had just arrived and were unloading timber from the truck.

"Everything OK, John?" asked Guy.

"No problems at all, come and see what progress has been made."

The floor had been laid and looked wonderful, solid oak boards a lovely shade of dark yellow.

They had marked out the rooms and it was now that any changes could be made. The area of the barn allowed for two medium sized bedrooms plus a larger guest room and en suite. A large bathroom which would allow for a free standing shower plus a big bath and a sink. A nice sized kitchen with a utility room attached for deep freezer and washer. The lounge had a nice views over the moor. There would be a living flame propane gas fire with a flue at roof level. Suspended ceiling would be fitted which would leave a roof void above, extra storage space if needed. At ground floor level they had a decent sized workshop, a small room that would eventually be converted into a gym and more storage space to the rear.

Guy was delighted. There was still plenty of garage space for the vehicles, and even room for a tractor and

Nemesis

snow plough if he could find a decent one second hand.

Back in the cottage Guy suddenly thought of something else. He had visited the cellar when first arrived but had taken no particular notice of it.

He opened the door to the stairs leading to the cellar.

It was empty but more importantly it was dry, there was no smell which would indicate damp, perfect for what he had in mind.

Right, he thought, wine racks along this wall and a big gun safe here. It was the perfect place to keep firearms, the secret room would still come in handy for illegal weapons but the police would want to look over where the shotguns etc., were stored. That brought another thought to his head, he would speak to Robert and see if he could expedite any request for gun licences.

Later that day he telephoned Robert who answered at once.

"Go six," he said meaning activate the phone's device assuring complete secrecy.

"Well done by the way Guy, Sir Ronald was delighted by the way you carried out the Belgium job, now what can I do for you?"

Guy explained about the shotguns and that they had to be made legal, he also mentioned the Luger brought back from Normandy.

"Does it take long to get permission?"

"Well you will not get permission for the pistol, but the shotguns and the .22 will be no bother. Look Guy, I would like you to have access to weapons, let's say some the police don't know about. There is very little chance that you could ever be compromised but it is better to be safe than sorry. Have you a place where any such firearms might be kept in secret?"

"Yes, as a matter of fact I have," replied Guy.

"Right then, this is what will happen, apply in the usual way to the police regarding .22, and shotguns. On Friday you will receive a visit from one of our people, he will give you a package, when you open it do so when you are alone."

Guy thanked Robert and grabbing his leather flight jacket made his way to the barn. Cox was throwing a small bag for the dogs to fetch and it was quite funny to watch them fighting over it.

"Next thing I'll do is fire the shotgun near the pups to get them used to the noise," he said.

"They're still too young but it's good they learn to fetch."

"I'm just going into town to see the police about the guns so I'll take the Daihatsu. I might buy a gun cabinet while I'm there."

*

The police asked a few questions about where the guns would be kept and Guy filled in a form stating he had no criminal convictions.

"Right sir" said the desk sergeant. "When you have the gun cabinets fixed one of us will inspect the site and then you should receive your gun licence."

Guy's next stop was a shop that sold guns and everything to do with shooting, living as he did in this part of the world country pursuits were common. He looked around before deciding on a large gun safe which would hold at least six guns.

Good job I brought the Daihatsu he thought 911s were not designed to carry large objects.

On his return Guy drilled holes in the cellar wall and fixed the gun safe with strong bolts, he also fitted a good lock to the cellar door.

That should satisfy the police he thought, he transferred the two shot guns and the .22 rifle to the safe and clipped them in place to the rack provided. The ammunition to fit all three guns he placed in the draws to the inside left of the cabinet, locking the safe he put the key on the same ring as the house keys in his pocket.

*

Friday afternoon a car pulled into the yard and a young man opened the boot and removed a package about five feet long. He rang the bell and presented the package to Guy.

"I think you are expecting this Sir" he said.

"Yes thank you, do I have to sign anything?"

"No Sir I had your photograph faxed through."

With that he got in the car and drove off. Guy placed the package on the kitchen table and slid a knife along the seam opening the long box.

Nemesis

The contents took his breath away, two Beretta .38 pistols and ammunition, the second object was a Remington 870, 12 gauge pump shotgun with a synthetic stock. This was a real killer and the police would most certainly not be prepared to grant a licence for either weapons, Guy realized now why Robert had asked about a concealed room.

*

Sunday morning, after breakfast Guy strolled around the property with Cox in attendance, the builders were not working and all was peaceful and quiet.

"It might be a good time to check the pups' reaction to the sound of a gun, what do you think sir?"

"Yes no time like the present, give it a go. I was intending you to have the spare keys for both the entrance and the gun cabinet" said Guy handing them over.

Cox came back with the shotgun and four cartridges, the dogs were running about in the yard as he loaded the gun.

Aiming into the air he fired one barrel, both pups stopped what they were doing and ran towards them.

"Well that didn't bother them."

He fired the second shot and apart from some excited barking they seemed quite content.

"That's good, some dogs are gun shy and will never be any use for hunting."

Cox set off to lock the guns up and Guy continued his walk to the barn.

14

Suddenly there was the sound of a car and a bright red Austin Healey pulled onto the yard with a squeal of brakes.

The driver was a very attractive woman in her mid thirties. She had short blond hair and was wearing a pair of jeans that looked as though they had being painted on.

Guy didn't know what to admire most, the sports car or the woman.

"She held out a slim hand and said

"Good morning, Lucinda Lane-Fox. I'm your nearest neighbour, thought it about time we met."

"Guy took her hand and said "Guy Bennett, how do you do. I must say that was some entrance, and by the way I love your car."

"She is a beauty isn't she? I could run a Bentley for what she's cost me."

"Can I interest you in a coffee, before I give you a tour of the old place?"

"Yes please, although I have been round the place before when your uncle was alive, he was a sweet old man and I'd visit from time to time to check on him."

"Well thank you for that, you knew him better than me. I have only the vaguest of memory. I must have been about three the only time we met."

Nemesis

They sat in the kitchen and Lucinda told Guy that she lived about two miles away in the old manor house. Her husband was a Barrister, a QC, no less, she had no children and kept two horses and was a member of the local hunt.

Guy talked about Marcia who was also a devout horse lover, and who on occasions went out with the hunt.

"I would love to meet her, does she live here?"

"Not at present, she is into sports management and that takes her all over the world. We are not married or even engaged come to that but we have known one another for about four years. Come on, I'll show you what I've done with the old place."

Lucinda complimented him on the alterations to the cottage, in particular the bathroom.

"Wait until you see the barn. My old batman from air force days works for me and we're making the upstairs into living quarters."

The dogs came rushing out to meet them and she thought they were lovely, stroking them and tickling their bellies.

Wouldn't mind some of that myself thought Guy, as he showed her round explaining where everything would be.

Finally after admiring each other's cars it was time to go.

"Guy I'm having a small dinner party next Saturday, would you be an angel and make up the guests? I feel awful asking but one of my old school friends will be staying with us and I'm a man short. I know it's short notice but it would give you a chance to meet a few of your neighbours and you would be doing me a great favour."

"Yes I will be pleased to come. It's not exactly a mad social whirl since I came up here and as you say I will meet your husband for one."

"Good, seven for eight Guy, black tie, look forward to seeing you then."

She accelerated out of the drive and roared down the road like Stirling Moss.

"Well what do you think of that?" he said as Cox came out of the barn.

"Seems very nice sir, I heard what she said about the dinner."

"Yes Cox, take me in the Daihatsu and pick me up after then I can have a drink. Don't think it will be a late do. When Marcia visits she will be able to borrow a horse, I think they might get on well."

Guy would have to visit Leeds again, he had promised to pick up his suit and blazer a week ago but had been so busy he had forgotten.

Next morning Guy set off for Leeds yet again, to be honest he was quite looking forward to the visit. Apart from picking up his order from the tailor he would enjoy another stroll around the city of his birth, it's amazing how many memories flooded back each time he came.

*

Nemesis

Mr Stankler came out of the back room where he kept all the bolts of cloth and did most of his work.

"I'm so sorry for not calling sooner" said Guy "I've been so busy with one thing and another"

"Don't worry Mr Guy, I have plenty to keep me busy, what's a week at my age?"

Guy tried on both garments which as always were perfect.

"Thank you Mr Stankler your a genius, see you soon."

I might as well take advantage and do some shopping now I'm here he thought.

He walked up one of the Victorian arcades stopping to buy three shirts and a pair of shoes. One of the finest shopping centres in England, without a doubt he thought.

He made his way to the car park and set off for home arriving late afternoon.

The workmen were still there and Guy looked to see the latest developments.

They were really cracking on, the rooms had been formed in timber and it was now clear how it would look when complete.

John appeared from the back and seeing Guy came up raising his eyebrow,

"Every thing is going well, we are almost at the point where you can choose bathroom fittings and such like. Could you spare a day when we can look at both bedroom, kitchen and bathroom all together?"

15

Saturday and Guy was looking forward to his dinner engagement. It would be good to meet other people and get acquainted with his neighbours.

After a day doing a few odd jobs Guy lay soaking in a hot bath, his dinner suit and shirt laid ready on the bed, he would ask Cox to help with his bow tie. He could never master the very last movement.

Cox had the Daihatsu ready by the front door as Guy slipped into the front passenger seat.

The venue was an old manor house, Georgian and standing in grounds, to the left of the main house an arch led into a cobbled yard with a stable block and a clock tower. Several expensive vehicles where parked in the circular drive. Good not the first to arrive thought Guy.

"See you about twelve I should think."

"Yes don't worry sir, I'll park in the drive and wait."

Guy rang the bell and was greeted by a butler dressed in a tail coat, very impressive he thought.

"Good evening Sir, the guests are in the drawing room if you would follow me."

He led the way across a spacious oak panelled hall. A suit of armour stood in one corner and several oil paintings of men in uniform hung from the walls. A set of double doors were open and Guy could hear laughter and the clink of glass inside.

As he entered the room, Lucinda came forward and took his hand.

"*Guy* how lovely to see you, come and meet everybody."

She moved towards a tall aristocratic looking man of about fifty and said

"Darling may I introduce you, Guy this is my husband Marcus."

He smiled as he shook hands, "Good to meet you Guy, glad you could make it."

"It's a pleasure, thank you for asking me."

"Come let me introduce you."

They did a circuit of the room shaking hands with the other guests, one was the doctor, the others seemed to be land owners or farmers.

"Let me get you a drink Guy what will it be?"

"Gin and tonic thank you" said Guy.

They went through the ritual of asking him what line he was in, Guy trotted out the cover story of consultant to a security firm.

Lucinda came up with a lady who was introduced as her old school chum Shirley,

"I will leave you to chat with Guy, whilst I go and see how cook is getting on."

"It was good of you to agree to be my escort this evening" said Shirley.

"Nonsense, it's my pleasure, I was so looking forward

meeting you all, I've been so busy getting the old house in order my social life has suffered."

Lucinda arrived to say dinner was to be served and could we please take your places.

Guy was sat between Shirley and the Doctor's wife who proved to be a good dinner companion and he found he was enjoying himself.

After an enjoyable meal they retired to the drawing room for more drinks and Guy found himself talking to Lucinda's husband.

"I am at York assizes next week, I always stay rather than face a long journey home each night."

"Is it a big case?" asked Guy.

"A murder, I am counsel for defence."

"Tell me," said Guy "I have often wondered how a lawyer can defend when they know that the client is guilty."

"The answer to that is they can't. If we know the defendant is guilty we can't lie to the court, but if it's just that the evidence points to the fact we can. Anyway, you are one of the first to know Guy but this will be my last case. I have being asked to become a Judge. The money's not as good but it will make a change."

Soon it was time to go, Guy made his goodbyes, shook hands with Marcus and kissed Lucinda's cheek.

"Thank you for a lovely evening."

Cox was waiting and they sped along the deserted road catching a fox in the headlights just before arriving home.

16

Next morning Guy was sitting in the kitchen drinking a coffee when the encrypted phone rang, go six was the instruction, Guy pressed the start button six times and read the message.

Subject. Abdul Mohammed Jibril.
ISIS Executioner. Age 28, height 5feet 8 inch, always armed.
Usually accompanied by Mohamed Asraf. Also armed.
Address. 65, Manningham Lane Bradford.
Attends Mosque Manningham.
Habits. Likes to play roulette, heavy betting at Casino.
Photograph enclosed.
Terminate.

The photograph showed an Asian man dressed in jeans and a leather jacket, around his neck was a heavy gold chain.

Not a devout Muslim thought Guy. There was additional information giving his recent history.

Subject disappeared from his usual haunts three years ago, was picked out on arrival to Turkey. Dropped off the radar again until identified in Syria two years ago.

Nemesis

Known to have joined ISIS. Became a commander. Took part in execution videos of an American Marine.

Identified by voice, took an active part in torture and beheading of several hostages.

Special branch arrested him on return to UK, released without charge due to lack of evidence.

One witness against him disappeared, presumed dead, without his testimony CPS, had no case.

Guy was deep in thought. How could he compile any kind of dossier concerning Jibril's movements? OK, he knew that he liked to gamble and most nights he would be in the Casino, but at what time? Would he be alone ?

The only way to find out was to get inside the Casino, but that presented a problem.

The law stated that to join a club of this type you were obliged to fill in a questionnaire and then wait for one week before being accepted. Was there a way around this?

The first thing I must do is visit Bradford he thought, then I will just have to wing it and see what happens. He packed a case containing all he would need for a week's stay, told Cox he would be away and then put his luggage in the boot of the Porsche.

*

On arrival in Bradford he parked the car as close as possible to the entrance of the multi story car park, it would be there for some time and in view of the attendant. He then walked on to the Norfolk Gardens Hotel and booked a room for one week. After dumping his case he looked for a car hire firm.

"I would like to hire a car for one week."

"Certainly sir, what had you in mind?"

"Anything as long as it's small."

He settled for a KIA Picanto in dark blue, paid in cash and drove to the address in Manningham.

Finding a spot he parked about one hundred yards from the Victorian house converted into flats where Jibril rented a second story apartment. He noticed a black BMW saloon parked outside, and was prepared to bet it belonged to Jibril. He took out a note pad and copied the regeneration number.

No point in sitting here all day on the off chance he will appear, so he set off to find a B&Q outlet.

His purchases included some electrical wire, a wooden broom handle, a small saw and a dark blue boiler suit. On the way out he found some rubber Croc shoes, the sort used for gardening.

In the car he removed the broom handle and cut two sections about six inch long, the remainder he put in a waste bin.

Back to the hotel, he sat in his room making the device he would use to kill Jibril.

Now time for lunch and relax until evening.

Nemesis

Nine pm, Guy found a Chinese restaurant and passed the time enjoying his food, no rush he thought.

Afterwards he drove to the car park adjacent to the Casino, parked the car then walked around searching for the BMW. He found it parked in the third row.

He checked his watch, 11pm, still a long wait. He sat in the rented car tuned the radio to a classic music channel then sat back and relaxed.

At twelve he got out of the car put on the boiler suit and rubber shoes, then got back in. He had really not decided if the time was right to make his move or simply to use tonight as a reconnaissance, but if the opportunity arose he would take it.

Around 1.30 am several people left the Casino and drove away – Jibril was not one of them. Then there he was and by himself.

It was too good an opportunity to pass up, he opened the car door, he had set the interior light to stay off. He moved quickly towards the BMW. Jabril was bending down trying the key in the lock.

The wire was around his neck in a flash and Guy placed his knee in the small of his back and pulled the garrotte back with all his strength.

Jabril tried to get his fingers into the wire but he had no chance. The wire as biting into his neck and blood was spurting out.

In seconds it was all over.

Guy removed the wire and placed it in a plastic bag.

Now back in the car and away before anybody else

Nemesis

came out, Jabril's body was partly hidden but anyone walking on that side would be sure to see it.

Guy drove carefully back to the city centre making sure to keep to the speed limit. He parked on the second floor of the multi story removed the boiler suit and rubber shoes and placed them in a bin liner.

He adjusted the interior light so it lit up and carefully checked his face for traces of blood. Satisfied, he placed the bin bag in the boot to be destroyed later.

He walked back to his hotel showered and helped himself to a whiskey from the mini bar. He put the TV. on not that he expected any news, maybe in the morning.

Getting in to bed he closed his eyes and thought *you got what you deserved you bastard* and was asleep in seconds.

*

Next morning after breakfast he approached the desk and told them that circumstances had changed and he no longer needed the room.

"No problem Sir."

He settled his bill plus the mini bar and returned to his room to pack.

The TV was on and a police Superintendent was speaking to reporters about the murder. It was not robbery he was saying, he had a gold chain around his neck, a Rolex watch and a wallet full of cash. He did not mention the method used to kill him.

Guy drove the hire car out of the city until he found a waste skip by the roadside, he deposited the bin bag

Nemesis

contain the boiler suit and shoes, dismantled the garrotte and put the pieces in another skip. He then went back to the car hire and told them he had no further need of it.

"We will have to charge for three days sir."

"No problem" said Guy.

He walked back to town picked his car up and set off for home.

An easy job as it turned out he thought.

17

Guy arrived home late morning, just in time for lunch.

"Anything happened while I've been away?"

"Nothing of importance sir, the building work is nearing completion and John wants you to pick out the bathroom suite and choose fitted wardrobes for the big bedroom."

"OK. I'll see him now. Is he on site?"

"Yes I saw him about twenty minutes ago, he's still here."

Guy went across to the barn and found John supervising the hanging of a door.

"You want me to choose some fittings I understand John?"

"Yes please Guy we're on the last lap now, work should be complete by next week."

They visited the show rooms together and Guy picked out a bathroom suite, fitted wardrobes and vanity unit for the guest room.

Thank God that's me finished thought Guy, although I must say I'm impressed. It's cost a packet but on the other hand the value of the property has doubled.

As he was returning to the house a DHL van pulled up, the driver opened the back doors and removed a box

Nemesis

about five feet long.

Ah, I know what that is. The swords and figurines I bought in Brussels. He signed the delivery note and placed the box on the table. He couldn't wait to see inside the package, a Polish Lancer and an Old Guard infantry man.

Marcia was always saying, *"Are you going to play with your soldiers tonight Guy?"* taking the mickey.

But it was a passion. He had started his collection about ten years ago and he now had thirty figurines correct in every detail. They were kept in the glass fronted cabinet he had installed with a light inside to display them. The other items in the package were the two sabres which would hang on the wall.

But first to business. He pressed the phone to activate the encryption device then typed the message.

Top Secret;- Mohamed Abdul Jibril.
Operation Completed. Termination Carried Out.
End of message. Nemesis.

He pressed the send button, and it was received at headquarters.

18

Right, now for some dinner, a few drinks and a quiet night in. Cox came in announced that dinner would be ready in half an hour, and could he have a word later.

So, a nice meal, a good bottle of red. He sat by the fire, glass in hand,

"You want a word Cox, what can I do for you?"

"Well Sir it's like this, I've met a lady. You know I keep going to the pub? She was working behind the bar, she is a widow her husband was killed in a car accident three years ago. Well, it's got serious now and I was thinking of asking her to marry me … But I wanted to be sure it was OK with you."

"Well, you sly old bugger, of course it's all right with me. Where does she live?"

"Well at the moment she lives with her father. He has retired from working at the farm and lives in a small cottage. If we were to marry we could live in the flat above the barn. She has no children and is unlikely to have any because I had the snip years ago, she is forty years old, a good cook and I thought she could do the cooking for you."

"Well I would love to meet her Cox. Why don't you ask her to dinner one night? I'll do one of my special meals."

Nemesis

"There is another thing sir, her dad is still fit and if we ever need an extra hand part time, he would fit the bill, he knows all about pigs."

"OK then, ask her to dinner, I'll look forward to it, by the way has your divorce sorted out yet?"

"Yes sir, all over and done with, I'd better ask her to marry me before I ask her to dinner. I've put the cart before the horse asking you first."

The introduction dinner was arranged for Wednesday. Guy insisted that he would prepare the food.

"Is there anything she doesn't like do you know?"

"To be honest sir I don't know, the only thing I've seen her eat is crisps in the pub."

"Well we can't give her crisps you fool, tell you what I'll play it safe with one of my steak and kidney pies, fruit and ice cream for dessert."

Guy spent the afternoon in the kitchen preparing vegetables and fussing around like a wet hen. Cox had never seen this side of him but appreciated the trouble he was taking to make the evening a success.

At 7.30 Cox set off in the Daihatsu to pick her up. Guy poured himself a drink and settled down in his chair.

He heard the Jeep pull up and went to the door to great his guest. Not knowing what to expect he was surprised to find a smart, good looking woman standing there.

"Sir, may I introduce my fiancée Betty?"

"Congratulations to you both, come inside Betty and let me fix you a drink, I think under the circumstances champagne is in order."

Guy popped the cork and poured three glasses.

"When is the happy day have you decided?"

"We thought the week before Christmas at the local registry office."

Guy found her a good conversationalist and they got on like a house on fire.

Dinner was a great success and she congratulated him on his pie.

"Thank you. I've decided when I came out here that I would do my best to learn to cook, I bought a few books on the subject and this was one of my first attempts."

After dinner they sat before the fire and Guy opened yet another bottle of red wine.

"I have a favour to ask Sir" said Cox. "Would you be my best man?"

"It would give me a great deal of pleasure Cox. Have you decided on a venue for the reception yet?"

"Yes" said Betty. "We have provisionally booked the village pub where I work part time, they have a nice restaurant."

"Right" said Guy, "my wedding gift is to pay for the reception and all the drinks afterwards. Is it top hat and tails or lounge suits?"

"I have given that some thought, do you think the RAF would object if we wore our uniforms?"

Nemesis

"If that's what you want I don't care if they do or not" said Guy. "You served with distinction and suffered a bad wound as a result, but no I don't think they would object at all."

Guy had been thinking about Cox wanting to marry in uniform, he made a call to his old CO, Group Captain Blount.

"Hello sir, Flight Lieutenant Guy Bennett."

"Guy how are you, no regrets about leaving the RAF, then?"

"None at all sir. Do you remember LAC Cox my batman?"

"Yes, wasn't he wounded during your last tour, I seem to remember he lost a leg.?"

"That's right sir. Well he works for me now and he's getting married just before Christmas. He asked me to be his best man and wants us to wear uniform. I was wondering sir if you would come as a surprise guest and wear your uniform, I know it would make his day?"

"Let me know the date and time and I will come with pleasure, see you then."

*

It was now early December, the building work was complete and and all rooms had been fully furnished. Cox had moved into the flat and made it his own. On occasions Betty had stayed over and Guy had found her an excellent cook. Both Cox and Betty had refused to accept any further payment although Guy thought that as she was now cook and housekeeper she ought to be paid. Guy had been introduced to Betty's father Seth. He had worked all his life in farming and was still fit and strong at sixty six.

Plans were now well advanced for the wedding which was to take place on December 22nd.

Just as the building work was coming to an end Guy had suddenly decided that he needed a dining room. So John the builder was called on yet again to build an extension which could be reached easily from the kitchen.

He visited an antique shop in Harrogate and purchased a Victorian dining table with eight matching chairs. Some of the oak floor boards were left over. Enough as it turned out for the dining room.

He had realized that as he had been invited to dine on three occasions since the initial one with Lucinda, once with the Doctor and twice with local farmers, it was only right that he should be in a position to entertain as well.

19

With this in mind he organized a house warming dinner for the fifteenth of December. Marcia was to arrive on that day, stay for the wedding and then spend Christmas.

Guy sent out the invitations, black tie, seven for eight. He asked Betty to call over and discuss the menu. Cox was to wait on table and Guy had bought a black jacket and striped trousers for him to wear.

After some thought the menu was agreed.

Prawn and Smoked Salmon Soup.
Mushroom Stuffed Aubergines.
Partridge in Wine with New Potatoes.
Vanilla Soufflé

Guy had been busy and had acquired a reasonable wine cellar stored in the new wine rack. So everything was ready.

He could hardly believe the difference in the place since he arrived. Marcia would be astonished.

Guy was just getting into the Porsche when Betty walked into the yard with the dogs who were now fully grown.

"If I were you Mr Guy I'd put that back and take the Jeep."

"Why do you say that Betty?"

"Well, I understand Miss Marcia is here for two weeks at least, and if it was me I'd have at least two big suitcases."

"I'll take your advice Betty. It's better to be safe than sorry it never occurred to me."

Guy parked in the station and within a few minutes the train arrived. He saw Marcia get off the train and wait as a young man struggled to remove two of the biggest suitcases he had ever seen. He rushed forward to help as the poor bloke manhandled both his and Marcia's luggage down the platform.

If she had been plain rather than drop dead gorgeous he wouldn't have been so keen to help thought Guy.

"Thank you ever so much" she said with a smile.

Guy gave her a big hug before taking over the task of wheeling the massive cases towards the Jeep.

Thank Christ I listened to Betty he thought.

"How did you manage to carry this lot?"

"Oh there's always a man who helps" she said straight faced.

Guy finally lifted the luggage into the Jeep.

"I was going to come in the Porsche" he said "until my housekeeper advised me against it."

"Well of course, women know these things, it's a sort of gift we are born with."

Off they went.

Nemesis

"By the way *Housekeeper?* Sounds very grand."

"You wouldn't believe it, my staff seems to get bigger every day, it started off with just me then Cox knocked on the door. Then he informed me he was getting married, then it turns out his wife's father is at a loose end. I don't know where it's going to end up, I really don't. The funny thing is there seems to be plenty of work for everyone."

On arrival he struggled once again with the suitcases until Cox came to lend a hand.

Marcia had met him before.

"How are you Cox?"

"Hello Miss, have you had lunch?"

"Hello Betty, thank you for advising Guy to take the Jeep to pick me up, they don't understand a woman's needs. And no, I haven't had anything since breakfast."

"I can do you a nice omelette or sandwiches if you prefer."

"A sandwich will be fine, I'll have a look round and then join you in the kitchen."

Guy took her on the grand tour and could tell she was impressed. The dogs greeted her like a long lost friend while Guy told her about tonight's dinner party and how much he looked forward to his first social event.

They sat in the kitchen eating ham sandwiches and drinking tea.

"How is the job Guy? I haven't seen Robert for ages but he told me you had joined him."

"It's OK, but I can't really talk about it."

"Why not Guy, its not dangerous is it? It's always been a bit of a mystery exactly what he does."

"Marcia, I really can't talk about exactly what this particular department of government does, it is not dangerous but it does involve secrecy. If my job comes up in conversation you must stick to the story that I'm a security consultant and leave it at that."

The guests were arriving and Guy was busy introducing Marcia and making sure that everybody had a drink in their hand. There was much admiration for the way the old house had been refurbished, and a particular interest in the Napoleonic figures displayed in the cabinet – at least from the men. Conversation flowed and everybody seemed to be having a good time. Lucinda and Marcia were discussing horses as Guy had expected.

There were two six foot Christmas trees, one in the lounge the other the dining room. They had been presented by one of the guests who grew them on his estate. Betty had been given the job of decorating them and they looked magnificent.

Cox entered and announced diner is served, they took their places around the table, Guy at one end Marcia the other.

The meal was a great success, Betty entering to be congratulated on the quality of the food.

Afterwards they sat and talked about the coming festivities, Marcia came up and said

Nemesis

"Lucinda has asked us to spend Christmas day and Boxing day as their guests, she has suggested that I join her for the hunt. Marcus has organized a rough shoot at the same time."

"That's fine with me. It will give Cox and Betty time by themselves to do what they want."

The last guests departed and Guy and Marcia retired, no sneaking down the corridor tonight. They had been apart for so long that their first time was pure lust and was over in what seemed like seconds, the second and third were a gradual improvement and the fourth at 7.30 in the morning was acclaimed by both.

The next day Guy suggested that they pay a visit to the Manor so Marcia could view the horses. She was whisked off to the stables whilst Marcus and Guy sat and talked about the new challenge of his being a Judge.

"It seems strange that I can't intervene and ask questions, but I can only act on what I hear from both the Crown prosecutor and the defending Barrister. And the worst part is when the jury retires and you get the feeling that they have no idea about anything they have heard."

"I thought you advised them what the the verdict should be."

"No Guy, many people think that, all a judge can do is sum up the points made by both counsel and condense as it were the salient facts for consideration. They often get it wrong and in some cases make a decision based

– 96 –

on if they like the appearance of one barrister over the other."

Guy considered how lucky he had been in deciding to live in the old house, things had worked out better than he could have imagined. He had taken to the country life, made many new friends and even enjoyed his job. Talking to Marcus about how juries came in with wrong verdicts enforced his belief that wrongdoers should not walk free due to either the skill of the Barrister or the stupidity of the jury.

20

The day of the wedding Guy dressed in his old uniform walked over to the barn, knocked on the door to be greeted by Cox, shoes bulled up to a gloss, uniform newly pressed, medal ribbons in place.

"Are you ready? I'll take Marcia in the Daihatsu with you. Then Seth can travel with Betty in the Wedding car."

Arriving at the registry office they drove right past.

"You missed it sir."

"Don't worry so much Cox" said Guy.

He continued driving until they arrived at a big hotel called the Saxonville. They entered and were shown to a large room with chairs at both sides of a red carpet. They walked the isle to take their place at the front.

Cox seeing the Group Captain sitting there in full uniform could hardly believe it. He stood and shook hands with Cox saying,

"Nice to see you looking so well, far better than when I saw you last."

Taking their places at the front they heard people entering and Cox turned around and said

"There's loads of our blokes all in uniform Sir how did they find out about it?"

More people entered and Cox turned around again.

Nemesis

"All the people from the pub are here, I don't understand it, how can they be here and provide a wedding breakfast at the same time?"

"Don't worry about it Cox, just enjoy your day, don't forget as your best man I've got a certain amount of authority to organize events too.

The tune *Here comes the bride* started to play and a bewildered looking Betty appeared on her father's arm. She wore a knee length cream dress with a matching short jacket and carried a small bouquet of flowers.

Guy and Cox stood as she arrived, Guy sat and the registrar asked who gives this woman to this man.

Her father passed her hand to Cox then he too sat down.

The ceremony complete the couple walked down the aisle smiling at the assembled guests, far more than either had expected. As they left the room they were received by a guard of honour from his old comrades.

They took their place in the receiving line to shake hands with the guests as waiters circulated with trays of sherry.

They both looked bewildered and when the landlord from the pub shook hands Cox said

"What's going on Bob? Thought you would be getting the meal organized."

"It's a surprise organized by your best man, just enjoy it both of you."

Nemesis

The manager appeared and told Guy that the meal was ready and would everybody take their place.

Entering the dining room they found one long table and six small tables with names indicating where people should sit.

After the meal the usual speeches were made, Guy told how he had asked the Group Captain to come and how they had found their old squadron back in the UK, and arranged for them to attend.

Cox was overcome to think that people had gone to so much trouble and could not thank them enough.

Betty's father told how he had been part of the deception and his daughter's reaction when they arrived at what she thought was the wrong place.

Afterwards a disc jockey arrived and there was dancing and more food, a very enjoyable day.

Cox said "I can't thank you enough sir, it is so very generous of you, *I must have the best boss in the world.*"

*

On Christmas Eve Guy drove the Porsche packed with all the things needed for a long weekend, dinner suit for him, two evening gowns for Marcia plus riding clothes for the hunt and all the other things women seemed to need.

On arrival they were shown into a large bedroom complete with a four poster bed and en suite bathroom. They left all the gear before going downstairs for afternoon tea.

Nemesis

After tea Lucinda asked if they would like a tour of the grounds she knew Marcia wanted to see the stables again.

Guy said he would like to see the horses too so he joined the girls leaving Marcus to study his forthcoming cases.

To the rear of the barn was a stream teaming with brown trout.

"Does Marcus fish ?" he asked.

"He does from time to time, you are always welcome to use it yourself Guy. I personally can't stand it."

They walked back to the house in order to get ready for the evening. Marcia was trying to decide which dress to wear, then it would be bathing and doing her hair. Guy reckoned a couple of hours at least so he settled down to read a Yorkshire Life Magazine.

The whole weekend flew past. Christmas Day Guy walked across the moor in order to get some exercise. Marcia helped groom the horses for the coming hunt. Marcus was still involved in his study.

Boxing day the girls appeared in their riding gear, always a turn on as far as Guy was concerned. They rode off to join the rest of the hunt and the men went out with the guns.

The beaters were local farm workers earning a few pounds on their day off. They brought dogs who were trained to retrieve game and Guy watched with interest wondering how his own dogs were coming along. They were now fully grown.

Nemesis

Guy managed a couple of pheasants and a large hare. He would take them home and Cox would prepare them for the table.

The ladies arrived back both flushed with excitement, the hounds had put up a fox but it managed to evade them, as was often the case.

After a cold lunch they thanked their hosts for a wonderful weekend, and made their way back home.

Marcia's visit was coming to an end. She talked about her plans for the future. She was to visit America, Canada, and most of Europe. This would involve being away for the next nine months. She loved her job and Guy knew he was being selfish but for the first time he wondered about their future. Since their first meeting five years before Guy could count their time together on one hand. It was the same old story, two successful people pursuing their own lifestyles seldom managed to stay together. He thought the world of her but to be honest he wanted more.

The day before her departure there was a strained atmosphere on both their parts and he knew she was having similar thoughts.

Guy drove her to the station to catch the one o'clock train. They both tried to lighten the moment but it hung in the air.

Guy managed to get a trolley and waited on the platform to help her board, when the train arrived he put both cases in the rack, kissed her and said have a safe journey, he noticed the tears in her eye, both knew it was over.

On the journey home Guy reflected and found that in a way he was relieved. It seemed to be a mutual decision rather than one of them being hurt.

Guy busied himself in the day to day running of his life. He asked Cox how the dogs were coming along.

"I would like you to see for yourself Sir"

They set off in the Daihatsu both dogs in a cage.

Arriving at a lonely spot on the moor they let them out and followed with the shot guns, they stood silently both dogs sitting by their side.

Suddenly a Pheasant rose up, Cox raised the gun and shot it in flight, it dropped about fifty yards away near a gorse bush.

Both dogs still sat until Cox said

"Get it Whiskey."

The black dog set off like a rocket and returned with the dead bird.

Soda never moved.

Seconds later another bird flew up, again Cox shot it and it fell to earth,

"Get it Soda" he said.

She set off picked up the bird and brought it back to his feet. Whiskey was still sitting immobile.

"If I hadn't seen what I just have I would not believe it. Well done Cox and well done you two" he said as he patted them both.

Nemesis

*

Back at the house Guy sat in his office checking his accounts when the encrypted phone rang.

21

"Hello Robert speaking, Guy I have some bad news I'm afraid. Do you remember an incident on your last tour when you were engaged in a fire fight in the local village?"

"Yes, I remember it well, it was on the way back to camp where Cox lost his leg to an IED."

"Yes, well, as you know you killed a terrorist in one of the houses, his wife was there with a young child."

"Yes, I remember she made a move to grab the terrorist's gun. One of my lads belted her or she would have shot the lot of us."

"Yes, well, the name of the terrorist was Mohammed Ashraf, he was a big player, trained in Pakistan. Our surveillance cameras at Waterloo picked up three Asians arriving on Eurostar. It turns out that one is the brother of the terrorist you killed. The other two are cousins. Our special branch people in Afghanistan have discovered that they are here to kill both you and Cox in revenge."

"Well Robert all I can say is it's a good job they don't know where we live."

"That's the problem Guy, *they do,* you may remember the local newspaper in Whitby took interest in the wedding because you were wearing uniforms? Well, a copy of the paper reached one of their family who lives in

Nemesis

Bradford. He recognized you and sent it to Afghanistan. You must take this seriously, they are coming for you."

"OK, Robert, thanks for the heads up, I will think about this and take precautions."

When he had finished talking he got on the intercom and called Cox.

"Can you come over right away, I'm in my office."

Cox came in a few minutes later, Guy filled him in on what Robert had said.

"My fault Sir, if I hadn't suggested wearing uniform we would be OK."

"No more your fault than mine Cox, you just don't realize that these buggers never forget, but not to worry now we know we will be ready for them. Might I suggest that Betty goes to live with her dad until we get this sorted?"

"You know sir, I would rather keep her with me if you don't mind, if those sods are clever enough to have found us who knows, they may know where her dad lives."

"Good thinking Cox, you're right Why don't you bring Seth here as well, but only after we have warned him about the possible danger."

"Right" said Guy. "Just wait here a second I have something for you." He opened the secret door behind the wardrobe and picked up a Beretta and a full clip of ammunition. He came back into the office and handed the gun to Cox.

"Jesus Sir where did that come from?"

"Don't ask. Just stick it in your belt and keep it with you day and night until this is over, and Cox I want you to listen very carefully do not be frightened to use that you will not be prosecuted I give you my word. The other thing I would do is to take one of the shotguns and cartridges and keep it handy, don't worry about me."

Seth came over later and Guy put him in the picture.

"The only thing we don't know is when they will come. The dogs are our best bet the minute they start barking will be our warning."

As night fell they made sure all doors and windows were locked. Guy slept with the Beretta under his pillow and the Remington lent against the wall.

Suddenly the sound of barking woke him, he looked at his watch just after 4am, he slipped out of bed he was fully dressed with trainers on his feet.

Picking up the Remington he pumped a cartridge into the breach, slid the pistol down his waste band and without turning on a light slipped out of the window. He crouched against the wall listening for any sound that would give them away.

Let them come to me. The one advantage I have is that they don't know we have been forewarned.

Suddenly Guy detected a movement, someone was creeping around the house looking for a way in. The dogs were quiet now possibly because Cox had taken them indoors.

The window that Guy had used was slightly open, the

Nemesis

man found it and gestured to his companion that he had found a way in.

Both men went up to the window, one started to quietly open it, Guy was not going to give any warning he stepped out from the wall and blasted both men. He pumped another shot into the breach and just to be sure fired again.

That takes care of you two. He waited again by the wall. No point in running about if you don't know where they are. He heard footsteps and saw the silhouette of a man but before he could react there were two gunshots almost together and the target fell to the ground.

That was Cox, he had double tapped the man just as he had been taught, one in the head one in the throat.

Guy walked out into the open. Cox came to join him.

"Well done. We won't be bothered by those three again."

Just then there was a flash of white and Betty came around the corner wearing just a night dress, there was a man twisting her arm and holding a pistol to her head.

A Yorkshire accented voice said

"Drop your guns and stand away. I'm going to kill this bitch as soon as she's seen me kill you just as my cousin's wife had to watch you kill her husband."

He levelled the pistol at Guy. His finger tight on the trigger. The blast of both barrels of a shotgun filled the air and the gun man pitched forward. What was left of his back still smoking.

Seth emerged from the darkness, the gun in his hand.

"Knew I'd come in handy. No one threatens my daughter and gets away with it."

Guy told Cox to take Betty back to bed and give her a strong drink,

"Have you any sleeping pills?"

"As a matter of fact I've some left from when I lost my leg."

"OK, make sure she takes one. She will feel better in the morning."

"Seth, you come with me."

They found some plastic garden waste bags and using two at a time placed the bodies inside and tied them with string, they put the bodies in the back of the terrorists van, threw in the weapons and backed it into the garage out of sight.

"Right Seth, go to bed and by the way thank you for saving my life, I should have known there would be a driver."

As soon he was alone he called Robert and told him the story.

"Go to bed Guy, leave the keys in the van. In the morning there will be no trace, it *never happened*."

Robert was as good as his word. To Guy's astonishment there was no sign of anything to do with the night's events.

Cox came over and entered the kitchen, Guy was sitting at the table coffee cup in hand.

"How about you?" he said holding up the cup.

Nemesis

"Yes please sir. I can't believe my eyes, I thought the police would be here and bodies lying all over the place."

"Ah well, you see it's knowing the right people to call in such circumstances" said Guy with a laugh.

"No really sir, how did you do it?"

"Look Cox, I'm not going to pretend, you're not a fool and you must have realized that what happened last night was out of the ordinary. I had hoped that I could do what I do and not involve you or Betty, but after last night you both must have many questions. I will tell you what I can, when I gave you the pistol you knew then that it was unusual for me to have guns laying about on the off chance that we would be attacked by baddies. I work for a government department that deals with ... shall we say ... *off the book problems*? Now I have taken you into my confidence, and I trust you not to say anything. We have a problem Cox, because both Betty and her dad know that ordinary people don't have the means to dispose of four bodies and a van, how do suggest we deal with that?"

"Well sir, before we turned in last night we sat, had a stiff drink and discussed what happened. As you say we're not daft and when you produced two pistols and a pump shotgun we knew that it was anything but normal. We also knew that if I hadn't suggested wearing uniforms last night would never have happened. What I'm trying to say Sir is, don't worry about any of us leaking information. I know that whatever you do would be above board and for the good. We all trust you completely."

"Cox, I thought I'd ask you first, but I've been thinking. Seth saved our bacon last night, I should have realized that the cousin who lived in Bradford would join the other three, if it hadn't been for him we would all be goners. Well, we have plenty of room here, I wondered if he'd like to live here in his own little flat, what do you think?"

"Betty would *love* that sir, and as I said before, he will be very useful doing odd jobs. I'm sure he'd be delighted."

"Right, ask him and sort it out between you. He will save on his rent and I'll fix him up with a few quid for the odd jobs. We all win."

22

Guy was sitting in his office when the encrypted phone rang, it was Robert.

"Guy, you will be getting a message in a few minutes, I thought I would just have a quick word first.

Was everything OK this morning, no trace of the bad men?"

"No trace at all Robert, thank you for your help, I had to tell Cox a little bit about what I do but I trust him implicitly. He won't say a thing."

"OK, Guy you should be getting the text now, I think we might need to discuss this particular job it's the most difficult one so far."

Tops Secret. Subject:- Igor Kozak ex. KGB.
Address 35, Park Lane. London.
The Gables. Northampton. His estate in the country.
Russian Mafia.
Known drug overlord. Also Arm's Dealer.
Runs Prostitution Racket bringing kidnapped women from old Soviet State'.
Chief Bodyguard Vladimir Todorov Ex, Spetsnaz.
At least ten other guards at both address.

Guy used the encrypted phone to speak with Robert.

Nemesis

"Tough nut to crack Guy" said Robert. "He is paranoid about security, surrounded *always* by several bodyguards. Todorov is the one to watch, he is a really bad bugger, always armed usually with MP5 9mm sub-machine guns. Do a surveillance on Kozak then get back to me."

Guy packed a bag, Cox dropped him at the station, he changed at Leeds for London Kings Cross.

He booked in at the Green Park Hotel once again, hailed a taxi to take him to Park Lane. Then strolled along until he came to number 35.

One look told him that it was impossible to carry out a hit. Kozak would be surrounded from the front door to the car and worst of all escape was impossible.

He checked out of the hotel next morning hired a car and drove to the address in Northampton. This turned out to be a large house in grounds, an eight foot wall topped with razor wire surrounded the property. To either side and to the rear there were fields so it was difficult to see more.

Guy thought if I take the next turn to the right I might be far enough back to see over the wall. This turned out to be true, he was on slightly higher ground which enabled him with powerful binoculars to see directly into the garden.

There was a large open air swimming pool with a pool house to one side containing a bar. The ground between the wall and the pool was completely open, no cover of any kind impossible to approach undetected. Guy estimated the distance from where he was standing to the garden to be at least 1,500 metres. On the far side was a dense wood again about 1,500 metres from the house. He watched as one of the guards walked out from behind the house. He was dressed in a dark suit and carried what looked like a MP5 sub-machine-gun.

Guy had seen enough. This was going to be a very difficult job. The protection team was US Presidential standard.

On his return home Guy telephoned Robert as requested.

"As far as I can see there is only one possibility, and that would be a long range sniper shot from the wooded area, and Robert, we are talking in excess of 1.500 metres."

"Do you feel confident at that distance Guy?"

"It would depend on the weapon. The best choice would be a Barrett .50, the problem with that is it's size, I can't just walk about with one of those."

"The more I think, I'm convinced it's a job for two, one to drop me as near as possible with the gun and all the gear I will need. Then it's make a hide and wait for an opportunity."

"Well, it's not a problem getting a driver, one of our SAS troopers can do that, tell you what Guy, I'll try to find out when he is likely to be there and I'll let you know. When the weather gets warmer he will be more inclined to take a swim, better for you too when there are more leaves on the trees to give you cover."

Guy was given the order to proceed. Kozak was expected to spend two weeks at his country residence starting on the 2nd, July. This information had been verified by the surveillance experts without letting the Russians know they were of interest.

Guy contacted Robert with a long list of equipment he would need, everything had to be fitted into a large waterproof Bergen. The Barrett rifle was 57" long, and weighed 29lb, this he would have to carry and it would have to done in darkness, for this reason he would wear night vision equipment. It was agreed that Guy would be picked up in a Ford transit van with blacked out windows, the driver would be an SAS trooper.

Guy booked an overnight stay at a Premier Inn. His story was that he was flying to Germany and would leave his car for one week and on his return spend one more night.

"That's no problem Sir" said the girl at reception, "but the car park will be charged at a daily rate."

Guy dressed in jeans, tee shirt and leather bomber jacket and met the van at a pre arranged spot. He changed in the back of the van, waterproof clothing and boots, and a specially made sniper camouflaged overall.

Whilst the van was on its way he carefully checked the Bergen to ensure he had everything needed for up to a week hiding in the woods.

During his service Guy had been sent on a course

Nemesis

run by the SAS on the art of concealment. During the Northern Ireland troubles the regiment had perfected the way to hide men in OP (Observation Posts) within yards of IRA arms dumps. The only thing the hiding men feared were dogs which could detect their scent and give the them away.

The van was drawing to a stop. Guy looked out to find complete darkness. He removed everything from the van and walked to the driver's door.

The SAS trooper lowered the window and pointed across the road to a broken tree.

"This is the spot for the pick up, just telephone and give me an exact time and I will be here, good luck Sir."

Guy gave him a thumbs up, shouldered the Bergen, picked up the Barrett and disappeared into the thick wood.

The night vision glasses turned night into day but with a slightly green tint. He made his way to the other side before searching for a place to bed down for the night. He found a dry spot beneath a bush, opened the Bergen and removed a sleeping bag.

At dawn Guy crawled to the edge of the wood. He needed an unobstructed sight of the garden. Having found one he crawled back into the undergrowth keeping the same line of sight. A large holly bush seemed to be his best option.

He made sure he still had a clear view from the centre of the bush and decided this was the spot for his OP. He set to work with an entrenching spade carefully removing sufficient earth to leave him a two foot deep hole, he lined the bottom with a plastic sheet leaving an entrance at the front and then covered the top with small branches weaving the exact same foliage as before through the gaps. He placed the Barrett in the hide and enough food and water to last a few days, he had decided to build another hide about two hundred yards away. This would be bigger and would be his LUP (Laying up position). In the event that he was compromised he would retreat to this hide and allow them to find the OP, hoping they would think he had pulled out.

Guy looked at his watch. 7.30am, things would be stirring soon.

He crawled back to the OP, looking for any sign of disturbed earth he was satisfied that all was well.

He settled in the hide ate two energy bars and drank some water, now the hardest part waiting.

He saw movement in the garden,one armed guard on his patrol. He quickly levelled the rifle and adjusted the sight concentrating on the targets head. The computer read out was 1,530 metre. Guy calculated that it would take approx 5.5 seconds for a bullet to travel that distance. There would also be bullet drop which would have to be taken into account.

He had decided to make it a head shot but if the drop was slightly more than he had allowed it would still kill, this type of round hitting a human body would be fatal wherever it hit.

Although it was a nice sunny day no one was tempted

Nemesis

to take a swim. He watched the comings and goings of the guards and on one occasion a gardener but no sign of Kozak.

As it got dark Guy made his way to the LUP, he ate more energy bars and drank more water, dreaming of red wine and rare steak fell asleep.

The next two days were more or less the same. Guy had begun to wonder if the information about Kozak being there was right.

On the third day Guy lay in the OP, binoculars trained on the house when two young women came out wearing next to nothing. They stretched out on the sun loungers, immediately removing the top half of their bikinis they began rubbing sun oil on one another.

Well, thought Guy it's better than watching the guards even though they have nice suits. But something told him to make ready just in case Kozak put in an appearance.

Minutes later Vladimir Todorov came out wearing a white bathrobe and sat talking to the girls. Then there he was dressed in a blue towelling robe, Kozak. He walked towards the pool and stripping his robe dived in to the applause of the girls. He swam up and down in a powerful crawl doing four laps before pulling himself out of the water by the side of Todorov.

Guy took careful aim through the magnifying sight of the rifle and squeezed the trigger.

Kozak's head blew apart as the .50 round travelling at 2.750 foot per second struck. Vladimir Todorv's white robe was covered in blood, brains and bone as the belated sound of the shot echoed around the valley.

The security detail ran out in force surrounding Todorov and pulled him into the house, the two girls ran shrieking to follow him.

Guy's long wait for the right moment to strike had not been wasted, he had originally thought the best method of escape was to take cover in LUP he had prepared. His big concern was if they had the foresight to bring dogs but thinking it through he had decided that he had about thirty minutes before they could get organized and travel the distance to the forest. He knew the only way was for them to employ some sort of transport and that he would hear them coming. He figured that if he made a run for it he could be a mile away before they arrived. With that in mind he had packed the Bergen with essential equipment the night before. The rifle would be heavy and awkward to carry but there was no particular need for a silent getaway.

He shouldered the Bergen, picked up the Barrett and set off at a fast trot keeping listening intently for any sound of engines.

He was almost to the main road when he heard the sound of motor cycles, three off road bikes tuned into the wood he could hear them slow down in order to negotiate the thick scrub. The next vehicle was a Range Rover, stopping on the road to drop a five man team all carrying sub machine guns, no dogs that was their mistake he thought.

Guy found a thick bush with a carpet of fallen leaves.

Nemesis

He rolled in covering himself as best he could. The five man team spread out and approached his hiding place, they were moving fast not bothering to search as they went along. Their instructions had been to get to the far side of the wood as fast as possible in order to trap him. As soon as they passed, Guy rose to his feet and continued towards the road. The Range Rover was parked where it had stopped and unbelievably was untended.

He was almost tempted to hot wire it and drive away but he thought there was a possibility it could have a tracker fitted so he stuck to his original plan of crossing the road and find a place to lay up where he could keep an eye on things.

He found a good spot and made a small hide He removed the Glock 19, and laid it down by his right hand just in case they showed more sense than they had up to now and decided to cross the road.

Looking at his watch he found that six hours had passed since the search team had entered the wood, it was now almost 3pm, plenty of daylight remaining. He tried to put himself in their minds, they either had found the hide or they had not. If they had they would then assume he had the time to reach the road and be picked up before their arrival. On reflection he decided that they had not yet found the OP, and still hoped to find him in residence.

A further four hours went by before the two motor cyclists drove out of the wood and returned to the house. Minutes later the team of five came out and collected around the Range Rover. There was a long conversation and much arm waving before all five got in the car. They sat there widows open, two got out and lit cigarettes there weapons laid carelessly on the bonnet.

Right, thought Guy, they have decided that I'm still in there and they intend to wait until I come out. Guy carefully retreated back into the wood and then keeping under cover started to walk back along the road.

If I can get two miles away I can be picked up and they can sit there for ever.

When he thought he had walked about two miles he got under cover and telephoned his lift out.

"I won't be where you dropped me. That place is compromised I will be approx two clicks further back. Arrange the pick up for 11pm, I will give you one flash on the torch when I hear you."

"OK, got you, expect me at your location at 10.56pm."

Guy crossed the road and concealed himself in the bracken, nibbled an energy bar, drank water from his canteen and settled down to wait.

At exactly 10.56, a black van drove towards him, one flash on the torch it stopped. The driver stayed in the cab. Guy quickly opened the rear door and entered throwing the Bergen and rifle in first. The driver did a quick three point turn then back down the road as fast as possible.

Guy changed in the back of the van, putting on the jeans and bomber jacket he had worn.

The SAS trooper dropped him off by a taxi stand

Nemesis

and Guy gave the driver the Premier Inn address. He checked in making sure not to stand too close to the receptionist. Four days without a shower made him stand out somewhat.

He booked a table in the restaurant for half an hour later then into his room for a shower and shave. He walked to his table feeling like a new man, ordered a bottle of red wine and the biggest steak they had. Then it was time for bed. He was fast asleep in seconds.

Guy checked out after breakfast, settled his account for two nights plus a weeks parking and set off for home. He arrived at eleven am, put the Porsche away and entered the house, he sat at his desk checked his answer phone and looked through the mail.

Nothing urgent, better get the report done now in case there are any questions. He picked up the encrypted phone, pressed the *on* button six times for complete security and entered the email.

Top Security.:- Mission complete, Igor Kozak Terminated.
Message ends.
Nemesis.

23

For once Guy found himself with nothing to do, he strolled across the yard and found Cox and Seth in what was to be the workshop. They had made a timber bench and fitted it with a vice. Seth had borrowed a small machine to turn over the ground where he was about to plant vegetables. They had also bought twenty chickens which were strutting around the hen coop.

"Fresh eggs in a day or two Sir."

"Well I must say you seem busy, any news whilst I've been gone."

"Nothing to report Sir" said Cox. "Seth has accepted your kind offer and we moved his stuff in with the trailer."

Guy walked back to the house feeling at a loose end, he made some coffee and was just about to turn on the TV, when he heard the familiar sound of the Austin Healey.

Lucinda walked into the kitchen dressed in jeans and a leather jacket.

"Hi, just on my way, thought I'd see if you wanted company."

"You must be clairvoyant, everybody is busy as hell and I feel like a spare part, have some coffee and talk to me."

Nemesis

"Well I'm on my way to Harewood House. There's a vintage sports car rally and show, every car since about 1930, The Austin Healey will take part, I go every year. You're very welcome to join me if you don't mind being driven by a woman."

"Love to, give me a tick while I change, I'll be back in a second." He rushed upstairs, changed into jeans and bomber jacket and escorted her to the car.

She drove fast and after a few miles Guy relaxed. She was a very good driver using the gears well and overtaking safely.

It took just over an hour to reach Harewood House. Officials wearing arm bands directed Lucinda to her spot.

They walked around admiring the cars on display, some over seventy years old, all in immaculate condition, their owners standing by proudly answering questions. There were also some cars for sale. Lucinda was saying they could be a good investment, but most of the owners just had them for fun and took part in rallies all over the world.

The rally didn't start until later so they found the restaurant and had a light lunch.

"How is Marcia?" asked Lucinda.

There was a pause before Guy replied.

"To be honest we are no longer together. It was a mutual decision, we hardly ever saw each other. Her job means she travels the world for months at a time."

"Oh, well I must say I'm not sorry Guy."

"I thought you two got on well" said Guy.

"Given different circumstances you're right."

Guy let that go by. He had no idea what she was talking about.

Lunch over they made their way back to the Healey and joined the procession around the Yorkshire dales. It was a lovely day and the top was down which always seems to make any journey more enjoyable.

On the way back Guy asked Lucinda what her plans were for the rest of the day.

"Nothing at all, a lonely meal by myself and then the TV."

"Right, it's about time I cooked you one of my special meals, nothing fancy we'll eat in the kitchen. You didn't know cooking was one of my hobbies did you?"

Arriving back home Guy settled her in the lounge while he set about preparing dinner. It was to be a seafood and pasta dish, one of his favourites. He opened a chilled bottle of Chardonnay, then went into the lounge and said

"Dinner is served madam."

Leading her into the kitchen he said

"I never thought to ask if you were allergic to sea food. Are you?"

"No, I love all sea food as it happens Guy."

They sat and talked about the meal and the day's

Nemesis

events him saying how nice it was to have been asked out and how much he had enjoyed it.

They went into the lounge, Guy put some classical music on and they sat and drank a fine old brandy.

Lucinda moved to sit next to him on the settee.

"I didn't understand what you meant about Marcia and you not getting on" said Guy.

She looked at him, put the brandy on the table, put her arms around his neck and kissed him, her tongue exploring his.

Guy would never say that he was slow on the uptake but although he had always found Lucinda very desirable he had never made any move in that direction.

It was too late now they were both locked in a powerful embrace that could only end one way.

He took her hand and led her upstairs. She slowly undressed until she was naked. Guy looked at her with amazement. She was breathtakingly beautiful.

He quickly stripped and they fell onto the bed touching and kissing until she rolled on her back, pulled him to her and said

"Now Guy, please now."

Although she was fully aroused and wet there seemed to be a certain amount of difficulty and he tried to be as gentle as he could, then he was inside her. She gave a little cry but said

"Don't stop."

It was over quickly and they lay there in each other's arms.

"You don't know how often I've thought about this moment Guy, now you know what I meant."

They made love again, this time much easier.

"Do you want to stay?" he asked.

"No Guy, I'll go home, I just want to lie in bed and think about how much I love you."

She dressed and she kissed him once more before driving off.

Guy lay in bed thinking. He liked Marcus and yet he had just made love to his wife. He knew that this was not a one off act of lust. She was not that sort of woman. Something was strange but he could not think what it could be. He knew however it would not end here.

The next morning Guy rang Lucinda at 9.30, there was no answer and the phone went into voice mail. He did not want to leave a message so he hung up. He tried again at 3.00pm but again it went to voice mail. He would wait until either she telephoned or answered when he rang.

He had an early dinner and was relaxing with a gin and tonic listening to a concert on the radio.

The doorbell rang. He opened to find Marcus standing there.

"Hello Guy, may I come in?"

Jesus thought Guy *this is all I need.*

Marcus came in and sat down.

Guy said "Would you like a drink?"

"Yes please, a whiskey and soda would be nice."

Nemesis

They sat there neither saying anything for a few moments until Marcus said

"We have to talk Guy."

Guy was just about to say how sorry he was when Marcus raised his hand to stop him.

"Lucinda has told me what happened. I don't want you to say anything, just listen. For years now I have owned a flat in York, I stay there when I appear in court. In fact, I spend more time there than I do at home. My lover of many years lives there as well."

Guy's eyebrows went up at this declaration.

"Lucinda has been aware of this and we have talked quite openly. She has always been loyal and has never mentioned the fact that I am in love with another man."

Guy started as if to say something but again Marcus held his hand up to stop him.

"No Guy, let me finish. This has to be said. When Lucinda and I married I did so in the mistaken belief that I could put my past life behind and live as a normal man and wife. Our wedding night was a disaster. You must believe me when I say that I found making love to a woman as distasteful as you would to a man. She has never complained and has been the perfect wife for an up and coming Barrister. We do in a way love each other but I have come to realize it's unfair to continue like this she deserves better. I knew that one day a man would come into our lives who would take her away and when I first met you I knew it had happened. I don't want you or her to feel guilty. It's *my* fault not yours. We have decided to divorce so she can live a normal life. I intend to be generous with the settlement and there will be no need for her to worry about money. I don't know what plans you have as far as she is concerned. It would give me pleasure if you were serious and I know the sort of man you are, but that is for you to decide, no pressure from either of us.

And now Guy, I will have another drink then say goodbye. I hope we can still be friends and I shall certainly keep a friendly eye on Lulu."

They shook hands. Guy said

"Thank you for being so honest and understanding and don't worry about Lucinda, I will look after her."

*

The next morning Guy dressed and went directly to the garage. He got into the Porsche, drove straight to the manor. He was not going to be put off by unanswered telephone calls. He parked right in front of the main door, opened it and walked in.

Lucinda was sitting at the kitchen table and looked up with surprise when she saw him.

"We need to speak right now Lucinda. Why didn't you answer my calls yesterday? I've been going mad thinking all sorts of things."

"I'm sorry Guy I was too embarrassed to talk to you after the way I behaved."

"Stop being silly Lucinda, you know Marcus came to the house last night?"

"Yes, that's what I mean, you don't deserve to be saddled with our problems, I'm so sorry."

"Well, *I'm* not sorry. I admired Marcus immensely for what he said. We had a really good talk and his final words were I hope we can still be friends, I hope so too.

Now I'll tell you what we're going to do tonight. I will ring Marcia and confirm what she knows already, but before I do that I'll ring the builder and tell him to build stables for two horses, one for yours and one for the horse I will buy for myself. I understand you will want to remain here for a short time because of the horse, but as soon as our stables are built I want you to come and live with me. Furthermore, as soon as the divorce is through I want you to be my wife, what do you say to all that?"

"You're sure this is not just a plot to get your hands on my Austin Healey?"

"Lucinda, I can honestly say I've never heard it called an Austin Healey before."

They sat and discussed how they could see one another on a regular basis without ruining her reputation as a married woman. Soon enough for others to know when the divorce became final. It was decided that she should visit Guy at the cottage, and on some occasions stop over, an excuse could always be made. Because of the staff employed at the manor it would be better if he kept away.

Guy returned home, he had much to organize.

He telephoned the builder and asked him to come and discuss the best place to build the stable block.

He also asked Seth if he would come down and talk to him.

Seth arrived looking worried.

"Is something wrong sir?"

"Not at all, I just wanted to talk to you about horses and stables in particular. I have it in mind to build a stable for two horses. I understand you have experience in matters equestrian?"

"Don't know about that sir, but I does know a lot about horses."

"Right then, tell me what would be needed, I have the builder coming soon so you stay with me and give advice as to size etcetera."

The door bell rang announcing the arrival of the builder. They walked around the property deciding on the best place to build.

"The back of the barn seems the best place Guy, there is access directly for the delivery of hay and such like and the trailer can get right to the stalls for mucking out."

"What do you think Seth?" asked Guy.

"Seems the best place Sir, I agree."

"Right, get on with it John. Do whatever you think to make it warm, lay on water and anything else we may need. Now Seth, I want you to be in charge of this project, you will be responsible for ordering all that's required for the well being of two animals. So I propose that I put you on the payroll for £100 per week, how

Nemesis

does that sound?"

"Well sir you have been so kind letting me stay here, I think it is more than generous, I will make sure they are always in top class condition."

After dinner that night Guy sat drinking a brandy.

I really will have to pluck up courage and telephone Marcia, he thought. He reached for his mobile and pressed the button.

The phone rang out and after a few seconds Marcia answered.

"Hello, it's Guy."

"Hello Guy, it's not often you ring when I'm away."

"No, well I've got to talk to you. Where are you by the way?"

"At the moment South Africa, but I fly to America in the morning."

There was a long silence.

"Guy I think I know why you rang, we both felt it at the station when we said goodbye. It's not working out is it?"

"No it's not Marcia, I think a lot of you but we are strangers, if we see each other once a year that's about it."

"I feel the same, I love you but I don't want to give up my work and that's not right."

"We will always be friends Marcia, I wish you all the very best and will always remember the times we spent together with affection."

Nemesis

Guy put the phone down and poured himself another brandy, he felt better now it was officially over. He picked up the intercom and called Cox.

"Could you come down and see me, I'll be in the office?"

Cox came down and said

"Is everything OK, sir, you look worried?"

"Everything is fine Cox there's just something I have to tell you."

Guy poured two large brandies and handing one to Cox asked him to sit down.

"You and I have known one another for a long time, and there is no one I trust more, what I am about to say is between you and me for the time being. You know I asked Seth to come down and discuss the building of some stables?"

"Yes I did sir, I wondered about that seeing we don't have a horse."

"Quite, well the reason is that in the very near future we will have *two* horses, and I will also have a wife. Not as you may think Marcia but another lady who you have met, I have fallen in love with Lucinda who is at present waiting for a divorce to become final. From time to time she will visit and it would be impossible to do so without you noticing, that is the reason I am telling you. I expect you to tell Betty and Seth. They would find out anyway but I ask you all to keep it secret until it can be properly announced."

"I can promise you that it will remain our secret

Nemesis

until such time as you tell me sir … and may I offer my congratulations to you both. She is a lovely lady."

Guy telephoned Lucinda and invited her to dinner "I have a lot to tell you, see you about 7.30."

The throaty sound of the Healey's exhaust told him that she had arrived, he opened the door, took her in his arms and kissed her passionately.

"Hello my love, how are things?" he said.

"Good, I've made excuses and told the staff not to expect me back so I'm *all yours*."

After a nice dinner and a good bottle of wine they relaxed in front of the fire, brandy in hand. Guy brought her up to date on Marcia and told her that Cox knew but was sworn to secrecy. The stables were organized as was a groom.

"So you see, I've not been idle."

"For my part I've spoken to Marcus, he intends to continue living at the manor but when it's over he will come out and live with his partner openly. He is being very good about everything. He's organized solicitors and thinks it won't be long before I'm free. Guy, would you like to visit my father and mother? I've had a word with daddy and told him the whole story. He had no idea that anything was wrong and was flabbergasted when he heard about Marcus. We could go down for the weekend on Friday and come back Monday, What do you think?"

"Yes, we will have to meet sooner or later, let's do it."

"Right we will go in my car, bring your dinner suit and clothes for three days."

"Can you give me some idea who he is and what he does so I can prepare?"

"Well, he is Lt. General JT. Wetherby, DSO, he is retired now of course.

"Oh, he does slightly out rank me but I'm sure I'll like him."

24

On **Friday morning** they set off for Dorset.

At the last minute they decided to take the Porsche 911, because it had slightly more room than the Healey and Lucinda like all women needed two cases. Guy promised to let her drive part of the way, the first time he had trusted anyone to do so.

They made good time and arrived at a pair of imposing ornate gates leading to a long drive. The name on the wall said *Wellersley House*.

The house was huge with stables and outbuildings, to the right was an entry to a row of garages.

"Just leave the car at the front" said Lucinda. "Someone will put it away when they bring in the luggage."

The huge front door opened and a butler appeared.

"Good to see you Miss Lucinda. Good afternoon Sir. Sir John is in his study Miss, I will inform him of your arrival. Lady Mary is in the conservatory if you would like to go through."

They made their way along a long, oak panelled hall hung with oil paintings of severe looking gentlemen in military uniforms. They entered a large glass structure where an elderly lady wearing a green baize apron was arranging flowers.

"Hello Mummy" said Lucinda. "May I introduce you to your prospective son in law Guy Bennett."

"I must apologise for that" said Guy, "I had intended to formally ask Sir John for his permission to marry Lucinda."

"Oh don't worry Guy, you will get used to Lucinda's rather forceful way. She's always being encouraged not to beat about the bush."

She stepped forward and kissed him on his cheek.

"It's nice to meet you and welcome to our family."

A tall distinguished gentleman entered the room, Guy took in his large Roman nose and piercing blue eyes.

"Good afternoon young man. You must be Guy. This has been rather sudden. We had never heard of you this time last week."

"How do you do sir" said Guy shaking hands. "I do apologise for the suddenness of the announcement. To be honest I think both Lucinda and I are just as surprised."

"Well, we'll talk about it over the weekend and get to know one another, in the meantime I think a glass of champagne is called for"

He rang the bell and the butler entered carrying a silver tray with four glasses and a bottle of Dom Perignon.

They raised their glasses and Sir John said

"Here's to Guy and Lucinda."

After a cold lunch they sat drinking coffee.

"I'll show you around Guy. Let the ladies talk and formulate plans. It's better we keep out of it."

Guy was shown round the house and garden.

Nemesis

"It's magnificent Sir." he said.

"Yes it's been in the family for two hundred years, all my ancestors were soldiers Guy as you will see from the paintings."

He looked at Guy and said

"Is everything all right, you seem a bit worried?"

"All is well as far as Lucinda and I are concerned but I do have a problem and I think I should tell you."

"Look Guy, why don't we go up to my study and have a talk?"

They entered the study and Sir John sat behind his desk indicating that Guy should sit opposite.

"The problem is my job Sir, I work for a Government department which to say the least is a little unusual. I love Lucinda and want us to marry but I feel she should know what I do but I can't tell her."

"Guy, when Lucinda telephoned me and told me the full story I used my influence as a retired General to make some enquires about you. I hope you don't mind but as a father I felt it my duty. I knew you had been an officer in the RAF, and I started there. As I was trawling through your records I came upon an old friend of mine, in fact this person was my second in command, who on my retirement succeeded me as head of department. That man is Sir Ronald Swift, a *small world* you could say. My daughter met and fell in love with a man who works in the very department I founded and set up in 1950. When we met I wondered if you would tell me exactly what you do. I knew that if I had been anything other

Nemesis

than a high ranking officer you would have said nothing. Now I can put your mind at rest. You have behaved like an officer and a gentleman and it does you credit that you worried about what your future wife would think, but I tell you now she will support you. I'm very pleased that my daughter had the good sense to fall in love with you Guy, now *let's join the ladies.*"

Lucinda and her mother were preoccupied with plans for a lavish wedding. Guy looked at Sir John who nodded knowing what he was about to say.

"When my man married recently he asked if he could do so in uniform, I saw no problem and we even invited our old CO and a few of his friends, also in uniform. Because it was slightly unusual the press arrived and photographs appeared in the newspapers. All this was done quite innocently but our addresses were published and the result was that it eventually came to the notice of the Taliban. They sent a team to Yorkshire to kill us. All this was because of our service in Afghanistan. Fortunately we got advance notice and steps were taken. I'm sure you know all about this Sir John?"

"Yes Guy, I do and I see where this is going. We can have the wedding here in our own chapel. What we *can't* do is make it a society do. This is the drawback of falling in love with a man who has served his country gallantly but by doing so became a marked man. I must say that my wife and I have suffered the similar problems from time to time, and we understand completely."

Nemesis

Lucinda walked across to Guy, kissed his cheek and said

"All I want is to be married to you. I'm proud of you as I always have been of daddy."

The weekend was a huge success. Guy admired Sir John and it was obvious that both parents were delighted at Lucinda's choice of husband.

All too soon it was time to leave.

The trip home was uneventful and they arrived mid afternoon. Cox met them as they parked the car.

"Good afternoon Sir and Madam. How was your trip?"

"Enjoyable thank you Cox, anything to report?"

"Nothing of importance Sir. The builder has marked out the area for the new stables if you would like to see?"

They looked behind the barn at the pegs marking out the new building.

"Seems OK to me. What do you think Lulu?"

"That's the first time you have called me Lulu ... I rather like it. Yes, in answer to your question the area for the stable seems good, better than the one at the manor."

They dined together and afterwards discussed the weekend.

"Mummy and Daddy think you are wonderful, I knew they would like you but they really went on and on about how pleased they were. I told them about Marcus, they had no idea, they still like him as I do but they agree I have every reason to end our marriage. Guy, I promised Daddy that I would never ask but I worry, how dangerous *is* your job?"

"In all truth it's not as bad as when I was in the air force. I ran more risk of being hurt then, as you know I was wounded and Cox lost a leg. The thing is, and this is unbelievably difficult to imagine, but I do the same thing your father did for years, he founded the department in which I work. Who knows, I might eventually follow him all the way and finish up running the whole show. But that is all I can tell you, from time to time I will have to go away and I don't want you worrying."

Lucinda stayed the night leaving after breakfast for the manor. The staff knew she had visited her parents and had no idea about Guy.

25

Two weeks after his return from Dorset Guy was sitting in his office when the phone rang, it was Robert.

"Hello Guy, got another job for you, details will be emailed giving all the info you need. This time it's one of ours, one of the GCHQ boys has been making a few bob selling secrets to the Ruskies, we would like it dealt with asap."

The encrypted telephone chimed and Guy read the information regarding the hit.

Top Secret:- Subject B.T. Barnes.
Age 59. Single, lives with partner LW. Simms. Male.
Holds a key position at GCHQ,
Body guards None.
Address. 61, Brooklands Crescent. Chelmsford.

This was a little different from the usual, this was one of ours who had betrayed his country for financial gain.

The information he had passed on could result in our agents being compromised and killed, Guy had no qualms about ending his miserable life.

He drove to Chelmsford to survey the area and decide the best method to complete the job.

Nemesis

The house was a pre war semi with a large garden, to the right was an attached garage with a wooden door a small passage way led to to the back garden.

Guy parked about two hundred yards away. There were several other cars parked on the street, no yellow lines or other restrictions, the street lamps cast a low light and there were no cameras. Guy knew that the target left work at about 7pm. His partner did not work at all and would most probably be in the house preparing a meal. Guy calculated that the journey home would take approx, thirty minutes.

Sure enough at 7.35 a car turned into the drive it stopped about six feet from the garage doors. The driver emerged from the vehicle, opened both doors wide before getting back in the car. He drove inside then closed the doors and entered the front door of the house.

Guy had decided on the method and time of the kill. He called in to an outdoors outfitters and bought a cheap plastic rain top with a hood.

At 7pm he parked the car a few blocks from Brooklands Crescent and walked towards the house.

Reaching the gate a glance round showed the coast to be be clear. He turned quickly into the drive and down the small passage way to the right of the garage. He put on the rain suit top and hood and slowly moved to the bottom of the passage, peering round the corner he was looking directly into a small kitchen where an elderly man was preparing dinner.

Nemesis

He checked his watch – 7.24 – time he moved to the front again.

The car swung into the drive as before. The driver opened both doors drove inside then came out bending to turn the key in the lock.

Suddenly there was an arm around his neck and he was pulled back into the passage, the knife plunged upwards into the gap in his rib cage and tore into his heart. He was dead before Guy lowered him to the ground.

Guy removed the plastic coat placing it in a small bag, he wiped the blade of the knife on the victim's coat and then checking that no one was around he walked calmly out and down the street.

He started the car and drove straight for the motorway and home.

On the way he stopped at a roadside skip and lifting the top rubbish he placed the rain suit underneath. He arrived home around 10.pm.

He placed the flick knife he had taken from the mugger back in the secret room, showered, ate a light meal then sat and had a few whiskeys before bed.

Next morning the usual message was sent.

Top Secret:- Subject BT. Barnes.
Termination carried out.
End of message.
Nemesis.

26

Three months had passed and the divorce was finalised, Lucinda was sitting in Guy's office discussing plans for the forthcoming wedding.

Marcus had been as good as his word and he settled the sum of £3 million, as a marriage settlement, which Lucinda thought was generous. He would continue to live at the manor as soon as the wedding took place.

A date was fixed for the the first of July, afterwards a cruise to the far east taking in Hong Kong, Singapore, and Thailand.

The actual wedding would be at Wellesley House the home of Lucinda's parents. They had a private chapel and the local vicar had been summoned to perform the ceremony. The guest list would be family and a few friends. The press would *not* be invited.

They travelled down to spend a few days with Lucinda's parents and to help with last minute problems if any. After dinner the first night Sir John asked if Guy would come to his study, they took a decanter of brandy and glasses.

"It's like being summoned to the head master's study" joked Guy, but he noticed that Sir John had a serious look on his face.

"Don't know how to start Guy but it's about your job. As I told you it was me who organized the original

Nemesis

department. Sir Ronald was my second in command. Winston Churchill was the prime minister at that time and you know how he regarded red tape. As far as I know the present Prime Minister knows nothing about what goes on, so we are in a position that Sir Ronald runs the whole show without reference to anybody. Now that's OK, as long as his orders are *lawful*, but who's to say they are – he could give instructions to have someone removed for *personal* reasons."

"*Good God* Sir don't tell me I've been killing people who have done no wrong?"

"I'm not saying that, but I don't like the way it's going. I heard some disturbing news the other day from a trusted source. You have heard of *British First*, of course?"

"Yes, that's the right wing party who have been outlawed, they are not allowed meetings and the police will arrest anyone who is a member."

"That's right, they are more dangerous than the real thing, they advocate concentration camps and gas ovens for anyone they consider to be '*inferior*'. That I understand means people of low intelligence, anyone who is incapacitated in some way, and of course Jews and blacks. As I say *worse than Hitler*, the thing is Guy I was told that Sir Ronald is not only a believer but is very high in the movement and even considered by some to be the leader.

When we worked together he often expressed the opinion that the time would come when those less than what he considered perfect would be eliminated. He made it appear that this was not something he believed in but that it was inevitable given the growing population."

"What are we to do?" said Guy. "And what about Robert, does he believe in this rubbish?"

"It's hard to think he knows nothing since he works so closely with Sir Ronald. This has really buggered things up, I don't know what to do."

"Right" said Guy. "Let's look at what we have here, nothing has changed in my relationship with Sir Ronald and Robert. Assuming they are guilty, meeting you is the only thing that's changed. Would that in itself make them suspicious?"

"Not really, I've been out of the game for so long and there is no way they could know that I've been warned about them."

"Another thing is that under normal circumstances I would never have revealed my role, it's only because I was worried about Lucinda that I mentioned it."

"Yes Guy, that's a good point, they must assume that I know nothing about your work. The best thing is to keep your head down and carry on as before. But *do* be careful, these people are *very* dangerous, if they ever got wind that you knew about them they would kill without hesitation."

"I need to see Robert in any case, I have an idea how I could suggest that I have right wing sympathies without raising suspicion."

27

The wedding day arrived, Guy and all the male guests resplendent in top hat and tails. His best man was an old friend from his RAF days.

The bride looked ravishing in a cream skirt and jacket, as it was her second marriage she felt a white dress was inappropriate.

The day was a complete success, the speeches were short and witty, the meal fantastic.

They spent their first night as man and wife at Wellesley House, flying off next morning to join their cruise ship in Hong Kong.

On their return Guy telephoned Robert and suggested a meeting in London. He travelled down by train and as usual booked in at the Green Park Hotel.

Robert came round the following morning and they sat in the lounge over a coffee.

"Why the meeting Guy, is everything OK, we usually do our business on the phone?"

"I wanted to see you as a matter of courtesy Robert, to explain about Marcia and I finishing."

"Nothing to do with me Guy, you don't need my permission to break up."

"I know that, but we have been friends for a long time and I felt it only right that not only you but Sir James and

Lady Pam deserve an explanation. Marcia's work means so much to her that we never saw one another from one year to the next, so we decided to end it."

"Well Guy it seems a long way to come just to tell me that, are you *sure* there's nothing wrong?"

"Well to tell the truth, I'm going to a meeting. The speaker is John Oxley the chap who is always going on about immigration, and how it should be stopped."

"I was not aware you were politically motivated Guy, how long have you felt this way?"

"A long time Robert, I saw how things were when I was in the RAF. People where allowed into this country and the next thing they were making bombs and fighting for ISIS. I lost a lot of good young men to these bastards. We must be crazy to allow it. It's time the people stood up for themselves, we have listened to these dammed left wing sods for far too long.

Sorry Robert, I'm going on a bit. Don't tell Sir Ronald about this, it just makes me mad. They must laugh at us giving them money and houses so they can make more kids to one day wear an explosive vest."

"Don't worry Guy, it will be *our* secret. You are perfectly entitled to express your opinion, after all you and I have fought for our country."

28

Two weeks had passed since his trip to London, he would have liked to to talk to Sir John and to tell him how he had sowed a few seeds but he did not trust the telephone.

The stable block was now finished and Lucinda's horse had been moved to it's new home. Lucinda with the help of Guy and Cox had completed the move and Marcus had once again taken up residence at the manor.

Guy was sitting with his after dinner drink when the telephone rang.

"Hello Guy it's Robert, how did your meeting go?"

"Hi, Robert, yes it went well he's a good speaker and what he says makes sense to me, just a pity we can't convince the great unwashed to think the same"

"Guy I've been giving it some thought, how would you like to attend another meeting in London on the same theme. This meeting is not easy to gain entry but I can vouch for you. What do you think?"

"Sounds good. When is it?

"It's this Saturday, a bit short notice but if you can make it I think you will be impressed."

"Well I've nothing on I suppose I could come down. Shall I stay at the Green Park again?"

"No come to my place. I will give you the address, stay the weekend."

"OK, Robert see you on Saturday about 9 pm I would think"

The minute the call ended Guy thought bingo! I've done it, I must talk with Sir John but how? He decided to ask Lucinda if she had any ideas on how to contact her father without running the risk of being overheard.

"I don't like this, Guy. Why should someone eavesdrop on your conversation with Daddy?"

"Never mind why Lucinda, can it be arranged? You will just have to trust me when I say that there is a small possibility that there is a tap on the phone."

It was arranged that Sir John would be at the local pub at nine pm, and that Guy would ring him from a public phone.

Guy took the Porsche and drove to the Golf Club where he knew there was a public phone that afforded privacy. At the appointed time he rang the number Lucinda had given him and Sir John answered. Guy brought him up to date with his efforts to gain entry to a meeting, and explained that he was staying with Robert.

"Be careful Guy, take no chances and don't appear too keen to embrace the movement. They will only give so much information until they are certain you're genuine. Keep this number and if you want to speak to me ask Lucinda to ring and say *how is Aunty Alice* during the conversation, I will be at the pub the next night at nine."

*

Nemesis

Guy travelled down by train and took a cab to Robert's home, his wife greeted him at the door saying it must be years since we last saw you.

Robert filled him in on the coming event.

"It's not an open meeting and only people who are members or vouched for will be allowed in."

Saturday evening they arrived in Robert's car to a large house standing in grounds. After parking they moved to the door where four thuggish looking men were examining what looked like passes.

"Just stay with me," said Robert.

One of the men came and looked at the paper and nodded to the other three to let them pass.

On entering the room Guy saw rows of chairs and a raised platform at one end with a table covered with the Union Flag. The room was full, not one empty chair which gave the impression that this was a strictly by invitation only. After a short interval a party of four men took their seats on the podium.

They spoke in turn predictably about the unchecked immigration policy which apparently was the cause of all our troubles, the Jews were fleecing us right and left and let us not forget the lazy good for nothings who sit on their are bums whilst hard working folks pay extortionate amounts of tax to support them. The way to stop this was quite clear. Anyone with an IQ of less than 130 would be sterilized so as not to produce more idiots to roam the streets. The blacks and Asians could do one of two things, go back to their own countries or suffer the

Nemesis

consequences which would include no handouts of any kind, no free national health and their houses would be inspected to ensure they were kept clean. Drug dealers and murderers would be executed, drug addicts would be imprisoned and denied any form of medication until either they were cured or died.

All these proposals went down well with applause for the more drastic solutions.

After the meeting drinks were served in a large room supervised by more shaven headed men with bulging biceps.

Guy was introduced to the panel as a war hero who had been wounded in the service of his country but had finally had enough of the stupid politicians.

They discussed his service and asked his opinion on the way the troops had been used. He noticed no one asked what he thought about their talk.

Their questions seemed harmless but on reflection Guy realised he was dealing with very clever men.

They know that attempts would be made to infiltrate the movement by British security and they would not be taken in easily.

On the way home Robert continued to ask pointed questions, he too remained unconvinced of Guy's sincerity.

The morning after, the interview went on during breakfast. It was done very carefully. Guy decided the best way would be to criticize certain points rather than

Nemesis

to appear too eager to embrace wholeheartedly everything that had been said.

This put Robert on the defensive trying to justify the more extreme views. Guy pretended to accept Robert's argument nodding his head as if conceding the point.

On the way to the railway station Guy felt reasonably pleased with his performance. He had known from the start that this was only the first round but the ball was now in Robert's court ... it would be interesting to see what came next.

It was not long in coming, Robert rang on the encrypted telephone and warned Guy about another job the details of which would be sent in the usual way.

Top secret. Subject. AR. Thompson. MP.
Age 50, Address 49, Greenland Drive Winchester.
Married. BL. Thompson, wife occupation High School Teacher.
Terminate asap.
Message Ends.

Guy opened *who's who* and checked for for details on AR. Thompson MP.

He was a Labour front bench MP, known for his outspoken views on immigration and free movement of people. He was very much a left winger holding public meetings and appearing on TV at every opportunity. He criticized the Government in virtually everything it tried to do, opponents accused him of being a Communist and rather than being upset he wore that badge with pride.

Lucinda telephoned her father and during the conversation asks after Aunt Alice.

*

At nine the next day Guy rang the pub and Sir John answered at once.

Guy quickly explained the facts and asked Sir John if they could meet.

"I have a plan which might work but it would require the cooperation of many influential people."

Sir John had a friend with a private aeroplane, he suggested he fly to Leeds Bradford Airport next day if Guy could pick him up.

Guy waited for Sir John to clear customs, they then went upstairs to the café and sat at a quiet table where they could talk.

"This is my plan" said Guy. "In the next three days I would normally carry out the hit. In this case I am convinced that this is simply to get rid of someone who disagrees with the British First party. What I propose is that this Gentleman *disappears* and is kept away from the media and even his wife, he would have to agree and people very high up would have to be in on the deception. I know it's asking a lot but it must appear as if he has been killed. If his wife can be trusted to act the part all well and good, tell her in advance. But I think it best that she really believes he is dead. He will have to be kept somewhere for as long as it takes, my best estimate would be six months. I know he's the kind of man who will argue against this but the alternative is that he might *really* be killed."

Sir John listened to Guy, he shook his head.

"I don't think he will stand for this, it's just too complicated and he will be out of action as an MP for an indefinite period. Even if we told him that by doing this we could put an end to the British First party, remember if we can't convince him I'm finished, and all we have done is for nothing."

"I can't just say I'm not doing this, the game will be up, and I will be a marked man …I could of course carry out the hit as ordered, what do you think of that?"

"No, leave it with me I'll see what can be done, I agree with you Guy there really is no other way."

Sir John flew back home and Guy simply had to wait and see what the outcome would be. They had set him up nicely. This was their way of proving his loyalty behind question.

Over a week had passed and still no news from Sir John. Guy knew that sooner or later he would be expected to carry out his orders and he had no idea how things would work out.

The bell rang and Lucinda answered the door, he heard her say "Daddy what are you doing here?"

"Long story Lulu, is Guy in? It's him I have come to see."

Nemesis

Lucinda showed him in to Guy's office.

"Hello Sir, Lulu can you fix us drinks love then leave us to talk?"

"Well Guy it's all fixed but not without a great deal of trouble. First of all I contacted the Leader of the opposition and told him the problem, he then organized a meeting with Thompson and his wife. You can imagine their reaction when they were told what we wanted them to do. Fortunately it was easier that I first thought, Thompson has an ego bigger than Everest, he was promised a seat on the front bench on his return, and he insisted that he takes credit for destroying the British First party. Apparently he has ambitions to be the next leader and he feels that being considered a hero makes it a certainty. His only condition was that his wife knows that he is not dead. I don't like it because she will have to act the part of the grieving widow at the funeral but she thinks she can carry it off. The Yanks have agreed to take Thompson into their witness protection programme for as long as needed and they did not ask why.

So it's all done, may I ask how you intend to carry out the hit?"

"I thought a hit and run outside his house. I can steal a car, bump the front against a tree to give the impression of hitting someone and then burn it out as near to the scene as possible."

"Good idea, for my part I have a body of a homeless man who was due to go to an unmarked grave, he will be cremated as Thompson. When do you intend to carry out the hit?"

"Two days from now if everybody can get organized in that time."

"Good, only one more thing Guy, I had to involve MI5, to smooth the way over things like the identification of the body, the death certificate etc., it would be impossible to do otherwise. But they have no idea about you, your name will not be mentioned ever, so what do you think, have we covered everything?"

They ate dinner cooked by Lulu, Sir John agreed to stay the night so they sat in the kitchen over coffee and brandy and talked.

Lulu was not easily put off and insisted that she be told what was going on."

It was Sir John who finally said

"Look you are aware that Guy is involved in a top secret department of government, just as I was when you were little? We have a rule in our line of work which is *Need to know*. This is done to protect every person involved, you must accept that we *can't* and *won't* tell you because it is not your concern. All we ask is that you trust us to do the right thing, and be proud that your husband is doing it for his country.

And now, if you will excuse me I would like to go to bed, it's been a long day and I'm not as young as I was."

29

Guy drove to Manchester and did a general survey of the area exactly like he would have done for real.

Later he hot wired an old Ford Capri and put a can filled with petrol in the boot. He then found a small tree stump and bumped the front end to make it look as if it had been in an accident.

He drove around until he came to some waste ground and after dowsing the car with petrol set it on fire and walked away.

He drove home arriving at midnight and went upstairs to bed.

Next morning he sent the usual message on the encrypted phone.

**Top Secret:- Operation Completed. Thompson Terminated.
Message Ends.**

Nemesis

Guy sat at the kitchen table watching the TV. The news was all about an MP who had been killed in a hit and run accident outside his house. It went on to say police had found a burnt out car in the vicinity thought to have been involved and were continuing their investigations.

Suddenly the encrypted phone rang.

"Hello Guy, Robert here, just to say well done for the Thompson opp. What a good idea to make it look like a hit and run, I'll be in touch soon there is a get together coming up."

30

Guy was looking forward to being home for a while, he felt sorry for Lulu. She seemed to have been neglected lately. But for the foreseeable future he had nothing to do. His birthday was next week and he asked Lulu if she fancied a few days away, but she said no she would rather stay home.

Rather unusual he thought, then forgot all about it.

Things were going well at the house, the hens were laying, Seth had cultivated the spare land and they had all the fresh vegetables they needed. Cox had been out on the moor with the dogs and shot enough game to last for weeks.

Lulu and Betty had planned a dinner party for his birthday. That's why she wanted to stay at home he thought. It would be the first social evening since her separation from Marcus and he supposed the locals would be dying to know all about it.

Guy decided to take the dogs out himself, Cox came as well in case they didn't react to Guy, but they obeyed every order and enjoyed every minute.

The day before his birthday Lulu suggested they go to Harrogate and visit the antique shop. There were one or two things she wanted to look at. They went in the Austin Healey with the top down.

Nemesis

They fell in love with a grandmother case clock,and bought it on the spot.

"If we had brought the Daihatsu we could have got it home."

As it was they settled on it being delivered the next week.

Home for a quiet dinner.

Guy had the feeling something was not right.

"I'll just go and see Cox."

"No Guy don't leave me. Let's just have a quiet drink and early to bed. It will be a late do tomorrow.

The next morning after breakfast Lulu said

"I think I fancy a ride Guy, will you come and see me off?"

"Yes, I'll just get my coat."

Lulu had already gone around to the stable and Guy followed a little miffed that she had not even wished him a happy birthday. As he arrived Lulu was just about to mount up.

"Oh Guy be a love and fetch my crop. It's in the stall."

He entered the stable and in the first stall was a large grey horse with a blue bow around his neck.

"Happy birthday darling" she said as Cox, Betty and Seth appeared round the corner.

"Happy birthday boss" said Cox, and Betty gave gave him a shy kiss.

Seth handed Guy a beautiful leather riding crop with a silver knob on the handle.

"This is from all three of us Mr Guy, happy birthday Sir."

"Well thank you all very much it's lovely, and what a surprise.

"And thank you my darling, I know now why you were so keen to get me out of the house yesterday. He's magnificent. How big is he?"

"Seventeen hands, but he's as gentle as a lamb, so I'm told. What are you going to call him?"

Guy thought for a moment then seemed to get inspiration.

"I'm going to call him Astra which is Latin for star."

They walked back to the house and over a coffee Lulu said

"And now we are going into town to buy your riding outfit, drink up."

Guy chose cream jodhpurs and a pair of knee high leather boots.

"My old leather flying jacket will be OK when I'm riding."

"*Oh no it won't*, you can't roll up in an old flying jacket, what would the master say?"

"Oh, I'm joining the hunt as well am I?"

"Of course you are my darling, you must take your place in local society."

He finished up buying a black hunt coat and a helmet with a black velvet cover. His final purchase on Lulu's instructions was a cream stock.

Nemesis

"Well, I certainly look the part now, better get on with the lessons ASAP, so I don't show you up by falling off. I'm joking of course, I have ridden in the past but I still have a lot to learn."

The lessons started next day. Lulu was a hard taskmaster and kept him at it for the whole morning.

"I feel as if I have been carting the horse rather than the other way round, I'm as stiff as a boot."

"Let's have a sauna" said Lulu. "That's the thing to get you right."

She had a funny look and Guy wondered if a sauna was the only thing she had in mind.

He was right and came out of the sauna still stiff in every place but one.

"That's enough for the first day" said his contented wife. "Same again tomorrow?"

She was probably right, an intensive course of lessons was beginning to pay off and Lulu was pleased with his progress and Guy was enjoying the improvement.

The hunt was about to start again and Guy was encouraged to give it a go but not to take any risks like jumping over hedges.

"Just stay with me ... and do as I do" were the instructions.

The riders assembled at the local inn. A few hunt followers were there and would follow where possible in their cars. Unfortunately a group of protesters appeared carrying placards decrying the fact that we were intent on killing a lovely fox who had never done any harm.

Oh no? You should see the state of a chicken coop after a visit from Raynard, all killed and one taken to eat. Nevertheless, people have a right to voice their displeasure if they feel strongly about it. But as is usually the case the genuine objectors had been infiltrated by the rent a yob fraternity, they were here in abundance. Most were the worse for drink and determined to cause trouble.

They started by smacking the horses' hindquarters causing some to rear, one pulled Lulu's foot from the stirrup whilst his buddy yanked her from the saddle.

She crashed to the ground amongst cheers from the mob, Guy leapt from his horse and picked her up.

"I'm OK. Don't worry."

"YOU STUPID BASTARD!" said Guy to the hooligan. "She could have been *badly hurt*."

"Who are you calling a bastard?" said the yob.

He approached Guy with two of his pals standing directly in front of him.

Big mistake! The best way would be to surround him, he reached out to grab Guy's lapel and that was his second mistake.

Guy raised his leg and brought his foot down hard on one knee. You could hear the ligaments crack as he went down, his mate threw a punch with his right. Guy caught the hand bending it backwards until the man went down due to the pressure on his wrist. Guy slammed his

Nemesis

knee with some force on the point of his chin breaking several teeth in the process.

The third man if he had any sense would have left the scene but he decided instead to aim a punch to Guy's gut. Guy grabbed his arm and twisted it up and back, the bone snapped and the jagged end was sticking out near the elbow.

The cry of pain could have been heard in Whitby. All three of the ruffians were in distress and would need hospital treatment. The hunt master was also the local Magistrate and would make a first class witness if required.

Lulu was still shaken but insisted she was fit to carry on.

"Shall we go then master, I suppose someone will ring for the ambulance?"

"Who is that chap?" said one of the riders. "I wouldn't like him to fall out with me."

The chase went well, the fox managed to avoid the hounds. Nevertheless it was good to be out and Guy thoroughly enjoyed himself.

That evening as they enjoyed their dinner Lulu said

"I have never seen anything like it, you seemed so calm and confident I bet those men will think twice before attending another hunt.

*

Life went on, everybody seemed to be busy except Guy. I don't think I'm ready for a life of leisure. There was the riding of course, he was going out every morning now and he was becoming quite good.

Lulu decided he was ready to put the horse over the jumps. She started him off at two feet just to get the feeling, then increased the height bit by bit until he was clearing five foot with ease.

"I don't think there is any more I can teach you Guy, you just need to keep practising until it becomes natural."

31

Sitting in the office one morning the phone rang. Guy engaged the encryption transmitted over a secure link – it was Robert.

"Hi, another job for you Guy in Spain this time, details will be sent in the usual way you decide the method.

Top Secret.- Subject Donny. Walsh.
Nationality. British.
Address, The yacht Sundowner. Moored at Alicante Spain.
Status. Single but usually has girl friends on board.
Body Guard. Jason Green. Ex, British Para. Possibly armed.
Subject wanted on drug charges, recent trial at Old Bailey vacated when witness failed to attend, thought to have been taken care of.
Lives on board the boat during summer months.

Guy informed Lulu that he would be away for a week at most. He travelled to Leeds and visited the HSBC in Boar Lane.

He requested a visit to his safety deposit box and quoted the appropriate number.

He was led into the vault containing the boxes and the bank clerk having located his box and placing it on the table left, saying "Press the bell when you are finished Sir."

Guy opens the box and looked through the several passports picking one in the name of Eric Wolf a German. Each passport had the photograph of Guy in various disguises. He also removed a thousand Euros in fifties and a credit card in the name of Wolf.

He closed the box and pressed the bell, the clerk returned placed the box in its slot and showed him out.

Guy drove back home to pack and decide the method of travel.

He decided to go by Eurostar and to hire a car for the trip to Alicante.

Lulu drove him to the station, she was obviously worried and kept asking where he was going and for how long.

"Don't worry darling it's just a business trip a week at most I'll let you know when to pick me up."

Guy spent one night in London and after checking out returned to his room to become Eric Wolf. This consisted of a black wig and moustache and horn rimmed glasses.

He placed his room key on the desk as he left the hotel. He took a taxi to the station and boarded the first class compartment of the Eurostar.

On his arrival in Paris he hired a BMW 7 series for one week. The journey to Spain was a long one and a decent motor was essential.

Nemesis

Guy figured he would make one overnight stop on the way before booking in at Alicante.

He arrived at eight on the second day checking in at the Melia Sol which overlooks the harbour.

The next day he dressed in shorts and a Lacrosse shirt and strolled along the the side of the huge bay where hundreds of expensive boats of all sizes were moored.

It was his first visit to Alicante which is a beautiful city rivalling many on the Cote d'Azur. Most people simply thought of it as an air port which was a pity.

Guy walked around taking photographs with his mobile and acting like just any other tourist. He finally found the yacht in question moored stern first with an alloy bridge to allow entry, a notice proclaimed no shoes to be worn on deck.

Opposite was a café and restaurant. Guy sat and ordered a coffee keeping one eye on the boat.

No one seemed to be on board. It was now ten thirty and unless they were having a sleep in it was deserted.

He noticed several vehicles parked near many of the boats, but nothing in front of Sun Dancer, still far to risky to chance a visit.

This was going to be a difficult job. The chance of finding Walsh by himself was remote. He had no wish to hurt either the girl or indeed the body guard so an explosion at sea was ruled out.

On the second day he visited the café opposite the boat once again, this time a white Range Rover with

British plates was parked alongside. Guy glanced at his watch, 12.30. Suddenly there was movement.

Walsh and a young woman came up on deck and sat in the cockpit. They were both smartly dressed as though they intended to go out for lunch. The bodyguard appeared carrying a tray with glasses and a bottle of champagne. He filled two and placed them on the table before returning below. Walsh lit a cigarette and raised his glass in a toast.

Looks like a special day thought Guy, a birthday perhaps.

Walsh stood and offered his hand to the woman as they crossed the gangway to the pavement, they both walked off towards the town. No sign of the bodyguard it looked as though Walsh felt safe enough to go out unprotected.

Guy left a ten Euro note under the ashtray and followed at a discreet distance. It was only a short distance to the many bars and restaurants in that area.

They took an outside seat at a Tapas bar in the square and ordered from the menu, Guy thought it best that that he just walk past. He would return in about an hour and see where they went after the meal.

He strolled around window shopping keeping one eye on the bar from a distance.

Walsh asked for his bill and the couple rose and made their way back to the harbour. Guy took up position on one of the many public seats scattered around the harbour and racked his brain for some inspiration on

– 171 –

Nemesis

how to get the job done.

There was movement on deck again, all three moved towards the car. The woman was now dressed in jeans and a leather jacket. The bodyguard had a large case in his hand, it looked as though they were taking her to the airport.

Guy decided to have lunch and wait for their return. If the girl had gone it would make it a big difference.

One hour later the Range Rover returned and Walsh and the bodyguard went back on board. Guy decided to keep the boat under observation for the time being to see if they stayed on board or went back into town.

The two men sat in the cockpit and ate lunch after which they carried out a few small jobs coiling ropes and varnishing the door leading below. It began to look as though they were preparing to put to sea, hopefully for a short cruise. There was nothing he could do other than return to his hotel.

The next morning much to his relief the boat was back, and the Range Rover was still in place. Guy decided to bring matters to a conclusion ASAP. He could see little point in delaying any longer.

He returned to his hotel and prepared the things he would need. He laid out a black wet suit and fins, a diver's knife with an eight inch blade purchased from a sports shop, this had a sheath which could be fastened to his right leg below the knee. He also put a pick lock kit in a waterproof fanny bag in case the door to the cabins was locked. He somehow doubted it would be but better be prepared. The last item was a black ski mask, he would try to make it look like a robbery gone wrong. All items went into a holdall.

He walked out, retrieved his car from the park and drove out of Alicante to a restaurant he had found in the hills.

He ordered a light meal and one glass of wine, he sat and enjoyed the floor show Flamenco dancing, a young girl and a man the music was provided by a guitar and an empty box which was slapped by the singer using his hands. This apparently was how the Spanish Gypsies performed. It was authentic and very atmospheric.

Guy glanced at his watch, twelve midnight, early by Spanish customs, families seldom went out to eat dinner before ten, children included. He had planned his attack to be around four am, most would be either asleep or too drunk to notice by then.

Guy parked the car in a dark street adjacent to the harbour. He stripped and donned his wet suit, fastened the knife to his right leg, fanny bag around his waist and fins in hand made his way to the water.

He estimated he had to swim two hundred meters to reach the boat, no problem better than to try and enter from the road side as there were still one or two people about.

He reached the boat and very carefully pulled himself to deck level, he stopped and listened for any sound below, nothing.

He tried the hatch door and to his surprise found it

Nemesis

was locked, no problem thirty seconds later there was a small click and he was in.

Freeze and listen again, he could hear the sound of deep breathing from the cabin on the left, the bodyguards. The master cabin was forward, no lights or sounds. He opened the door a crack and peered in.

A double bed with one person sleeping, Walsh was laid on his back fast asleep. Guy removed the pillow on the other side and with one quick movement brought it down on the sleeping man's face and at the same time sticking the blade up into the heart. He kept the pillow in place but there was no need. Walsh died without uttering a sound.

To make it look like a break in Guy unclasped the Rolex watch from his wrist and picked up a bulging wallet from the dressing table, he placed both in the fanny bag. He would throw both away except for any cash in the wallet.

He listened again as he passed the bodyguard's door, still rhythmic breathing. This would not look good on his CV, thought Guy as he lowered himself into the sea.

On reaching the car he changed back into his normal clothes putting the wet suit and fins as well as the watch and wallet in the holdall, to be disposed of before leaving.

Guy walked into the hotel which was still busy with late arrivals. No one took any notice of him as he entered the lift. Once in his room he searched through the wallet and removed the cash which amounted to five hundred Euros. The credit cards he left in place. He looked at the watch, it was new and worth about twelve thousand pounds. He deliberated on whether to keep it or throw it away, it seemed a shame.

Guy had a long shower, a large whiskey from the mini bar then got into bed.

*

Guy sat over his breakfast coffee and ran the events of yesterday over in his mind, he had decided to stay one more day to minimize the risk of being stopped by a road block if indeed the Guardia did not buy the theory that the murder was the result of an interrupted robbery.

Later that day he had used the bank card from Walsh's wallet, not because he wanted the cash but he thought it would confirm that the death had been caused by some unsophisticated person who thought he could use the card without a pin number. The wallet and all the cards were then disposed of, he had thought long and hard about the Rolex and decided to risk keeping it. In the unlikely event that it was discovered on him he would say he bought it from a street vendor for fifty Euros, it was just too good to throw away.

The rest of the day was spent as a tourist, he sat in the café opposite Sun Dancer and watched the police taking fingerprints and examining the cabins, there was yellow tape all around the boat indicating a crime scene.

Nemesis

It was a big event in Alicante which has a low crime rate, the local police were picking up beggars and vagrants for questioning and the local radio station confirmed that this was their line of enquiry.

Guy checked out of his hotel the next morning took the A7 towards Paris, had one overnight stop and arrived mid day. He boarded the Euro Star, opened his newspaper and read until he drifted off to sleep. Arriving in the UK he booked an overnight stay near Kings Cross in his own name and caught the nine o'clock train to Leeds the next day.

He contacted Lulu on the way up and arranged for her to meet him at the station, she was waiting as he came off the platform.

"Hello darling how was your trip?"

"Uneventful really I suppose" replied Guy. "How are things at home, any news?"

"No very boring without you of course, I've been out riding every day I even took Astra to give him some exercise he's a wonderful horse I really like him. Father rang and asked after you."

"Did he leave any message? Does he want me to ring back?"

"He didn't say, there's more going on with you two. It's like the secret seven."

"Don't worry it's just now I work in his old department he likes to be in the know."

*

Guy sat in his office and prepared to send the usual confirmation that his instructions had been carried out successfully.

TOP SECRET:- Subject. D. Walsh.
Operation carried out.
Terminated.
Message ends.

Nemesis.

32

Guy was worried, he realized that what he had originally thought of as a government sponsored department was really nothing more that the private organization of Sir Ronald Swift. It was in fact arbitrary execution without judicial process and if things went pear shaped he would be left holding the baby. He decided that he must get in touch with Lulu's father and ask his advice, after all he was the originator of the whole thing.

Later after dinner they sat together in front of the fire.

"How do feel about a visit to your parents, it's ages since you last saw them?"

"Yes that's a great idea I'll give them a ring and say we will go down Friday and spend a few days."

Friday morning they set off in the Healey at Lulu's request.

"Do it good to have a long run" she said.

Guy had an idea that she was not fooled and knew the trip was because he wanted to speak to the General.

They arrived just in time for a late lunch. Guy always enjoyed his visits to Wellesley House. His father in law suggested they should have a talk later.

"Keep me informed about my old department."

They retired to his study and the General closed the door and took seat behind the large desk.

"What's wrong Guy I can tell you're worried?"

"I am *more* than worried Sir. I'm frightened to death. As I see it no one knows about the department except us and when things go wrong as they will. I'll be facing a murder charge. First of all I would like to know where the money for these operations comes from. I can't accept that Sir Ronald forks out the cash. It must take millions to operate an organization like this."

"You're quite right Guy, it's what is known as a *black opp*. It's off the book. Originally MI5 were responsible and probably still are, Churchill was the Prime minister but you can bet that the modern MPs wouldn't touch this with a barge pole."

"So where does this leave us, or – more importantly – *me?*"

"As I see it Guy no one will actually stand up and say I'm responsible, but if we can give them something in return they will protect you."

"What can I possibly give them?"

"You can give them the British First party, if we can persuade them that you are willing to go under cover and identify the leaders MI5 will take you under their wing. If you think about it you are already half way there over the business with the MP who you pretended to kill."

"Could you get an interview with the head of MI5 Sir?"

Nemesis

"Yes Guy, I think I can. You will have to be ready to come with me to their headquarters and put it before them. It's not without a great deal of danger to you. If these Nazi sympathizers suspect anything wrong they will kill you. Look Guy, after this weekend return home and wait for my call. I'll get on to it ASAP, and then we will pay a visit to MI5 and tell the whole story."

No more was said and Lulu relaxed thinking whatever had been bothering Guy had been sorted out during his conversation with her father.

They returned home on Monday and Guy did his best to appear settled. They went riding each morning and he took an interest in the daily running of the property.

He must have been mad to have taken the job in the first place but he had genuinely thought it was a government sponsored outfit albeit one that was so secret it could never be discussed.

A week later Sir John telephoned and they arranged a meeting in London for Wednesday morning.

This was to be held at Thames House the traditional home of MI5.

On the way to the meeting Sir John put Guy in the picture.

"We have passes and we will be shown directly the D G's office. She is not the easiest person in the world but just tell the truth and hope for the best."

They showed their passes and were directed to the lift which took them to the top floor, down a long corridor to a door marked secretary.

Nemesis

The woman who sat at the desk asked them to take a seat and she would tell the DG they had arrived, she pressed a button and spoke quietly into telephone.

"You may go straight in General. She's expecting you and opened a door leading to the DG's suite.

Guy was impressed, a large office with a window looking directly on to the Houses of Parliament, the DG sat behind a beautiful walnut desk. She stood and offered her hand to Sir John.

"Good to see you John, it's been along time, and this must be the young man in question?"

"Good to see you too Sandra, we go back a long way. Guy may I introduce you to Mrs Towers the Director General of MI5."

"Sit down won't you, it's a bit early for a drink but I'll organize some coffee, then Mr Bennett can tell me all about what he has been up to."

Guy started right from the beginning, how he had been offered a job by Sir Ronald and how he had been trained in street craft and disguises and how he had carried out various hits starting with the one in Belgium.

"Did it not seem a trifle unusual to be asked to kill people?"

"Well yes, when you put it like that it did but I agreed in principle with Sir Ronald when he told me people were literally getting away with murder due to The human rights law and the politically correct brigade. When I was serving in Afghanistan it was going on all the time, we knew who the bad men were but we couldn't touch

– 181 –

them for various reasons and my men were being killed. Now at first, all the people I was ordered to kill seemed to deserve it but when I was asked to kill an MP, I began to think is this right? It was then that I approached Sir John and we devised a plan to take him out of circulation and make out that he had been killed."

"Yes I know about that. In fact I know about all the kills you have carried out, between you and me you are right to assume that they all deserved what they got but you must realise that if the press got hold of this our feet wouldn't touch the ground. And this as Sir John will tell you is why we refer to these things as off the books *black operations*."

"So" said Guy, "What you are saying is that MI5 has known all about Sir Ronald's department and that it is funded by you?"

"You may *think* that but I couldn't possibly comment" said the director.

"For my part" said Guy "it was only when I found out about their connection to the British First Party that I realized I could be asked to kill perfectly innocent people."

"If we could identify the senior figures some of whom are in very influential positions in Government and I have also heard that one of the minor Royals is a member, it would be a major success."

She didn't have to say it would be a great thing for her personally.

"Robert has proposed me as a potential member

of the party, and has more or less said that it would be confirmed shortly."

"Are you prepared to work for us under cover? And be certain of one thing Guy, if you are found out they will have no hesitation about killing you."

"I understand the risks, and I'm quite ready to find out all I can and report back to you, I'm not even sure who the leader is. I suspect Sir Ronald but I have no proof at all and he certainly was not one of the guests at the dinner I went to. There is one major problem, what if I'm ordered to kill someone I know to be innocent? If I refuse, my cover is blown."

"That I agree is a problem, all I will say is if it happens we will deal with it. Now I propose that you report to Sir John. If he agrees, the fewer who know about this the better. Sorry to drop this on you John, I know you are retired. What do you say?"

"Yes I agree. Guy can report directly to me and I will keep you informed, but *to you only* Sandra. I'm not saying I don't trust your security but let's be honest some of your own people could be part of the British First Party."

On leaving Thames House they discussed the the outcome of the meeting in more detail.

"It seems to me that MI5 was aware from the start that I was hired as an assassin and it suited them to say nothing, but had things gone wrong I would be the one standing in the dock."

Nemesis

"That's the way it's done I'm afraid Guy, you are involved in a very dirty business but now to some extent you are *official*. Sandra would throw you to the wolves except that she now knows I am involved and is aware of my connections to the highest in the land. She would not dare to double cross you knowing I could blow her out of the water with one telephone call – that's why I insisted I report directly to her."

33

Guy returned to Yorkshire and normality if you could call it that. It was good to be home again and see Lulu. He was feeling guilty that she had been neglected.

They went out with the horses and enjoyed the freedom of the moor. She did not ask him about his trip to London. Guy felt that at last she accepted her role.

For the first time in months Guy relaxed, he had not realized how concerned he had been about the situation he was in, until the contract on Thompson MP. he had been quite content to carry out his orders.

But that particular job had brought home just how far he was out on a limb, he still had the problem of how to avoid killing an innocent person whilst still retaining the confidence of the department.

The encrypted phone rang.

"Hello Guy it's Robert. Good news, your application to join the party has been accepted and they have given you a position of authority rather than ordinary membership. We are having a meeting a week on Saturday at my father's house, I would like you to attend and I've arranged for you to stay the night is that OK?"

Nemesis

"Yes Robert, I can make that. Is there any dress code?"

"Black tie is the usual, I won't be staying all night but will see you about eight, arrive any time after lunch there both looking forward to your visit."

Well thought Guy, *Sir James and Lady Pamela! Who would have guessed they were part of an organization like that?*

A buffet dinner was served and many of the guests appeared to be the worse for drink. Several came up and introduced themselves and Guy recognized at least two members of Parliament and three giants of the media. Influential people who would never be suspected of such hatred. He made mental notes on anyone he recognized to be passed on by way of Sir John.

Robert came and said

"I'm away Guy I promised to go home, I understand you're staying the night?"

Most were leaving and Guy was ready for bed himself, he bid his hosts goodnight and made his way upstairs.

He lay thinking about the many times he had spent in this bed and how Marcia used to creep into his room, and within minutes he was asleep.

It must have been about three when the door silently opened and a woman entered dropping her dressing gown as she slid into his bed.

A hand was between his legs as she stroked him, slowly at first and then as he began to react faster.

Nemesis

Although he was asleep it wasn't long before he had a massive erection.

He suddenly woke up and started to say something.

"Shush" she said. *"Shush"* whilst still working her hand up and down. She threw her leg over him and sitting astride took him in her hand guiding him into her. She started rocking backwards and forwards, her vagina seemed to grip and slacken at her will. He was fully awake by now and in spite of himself he could not help enjoying the experience.

He exploded into her and at the same moment she gave a cry and shuddered to an organism.

"Marcia!" he said, "I didn't see you, when did you get here?"

She rolled off him and kissed his neck. A shaft of light played on her face and he recognized not Marcia but her mother. He had just screwed a sixty year old woman and had to admit it was the finest experience ever.

He always remembered one of his brother officers saying "You always get a better tune out of an old fiddle" – God he was right.

*

Lady Pam was already seated when Guy walked in to breakfast. Sir James said "Morning Guy did you sleep well?"

"Thank you yes, it took some time but I finally had it off."

Nemesis

He glanced at Lady Pam, who smiled at his deliberate misquote. After coffee Guy thanked his hosts, in particular Lady Pam, and made a quick start for home arriving at mid morning.

"Anything to report he asked."
"No just the same old routine."
"Look love, I know it's been bad for you just lately with me going away every week but I promise that things will change very soon, I can't say too much but this episode of my life is nearly over thank God."

As arranged Guy contacted Sir John with a list of members, many of whom held positions of influence in both government and media.

Sir John telephoned shortly afterwards using the secure phone provided by MI5.

"Sandra is delighted with your list of names and not a little surprised by some, keep it up we still have no idea who the leader is."

Robert rang a few days later inviting him to yet another social meeting this time to be held at Robert's home.

"Usual thing Guy, stay the night if you like, gives you the chance to enjoy a few drinks."

Making his excuses to Lulu yet again he decided to drive down. He arrived late afternoon and spent a couple of hours talking to Robert in his study.

"Any difference to the people I met at your father's. Do I get to meet the boss this time?"

Robert looked thoughtful.

"Is there any reason why you *want* to?"

Guy decided to be very careful. Was Robert suddenly suspicious of his questions.?

"No not really it's just that he is referred to as 'the leader' but no one ever mentions him by name, I suppose from a security point of view?"

"It's not that, the leader does often arrive out of the blue on occasions and if that happens I will introduce you with pleasure."

Guy retired to his bedroom to shower and change for the evening, the guests had started to arrive and drinks were served by young girls dressed in what looked like the outfits seen on the old news reels of Hitler youth, short black skirts, white shirts and back ties. Many wore their hair in twin plaits in the manner of the German female youth of the 1930s.

Guy was engaged in conversation with a member of parliament and a well known TV personality when he noticed the arrival of Sir Robert.

No one seemed to take much notice of him as he came across hand outstretched towards Guy's group.

"Hello Guy nice to see you again, I must congratulate you on the work you have carried out since we last met, I hope Robert passed on my admiration of your efforts?"

"Yes Sir, he always takes the time to ring me after a job and pass on your compliments."

Nemesis

"Good, I'm pleased you have seen fit to join our little band. It's really a continuation of our department in many ways. If our politicians had any guts it would never have been necessary to form our party in the first place. But as you know the Conservatives are getting softer and moving to the left, and as for the Labour party and the Liberals we might as well *give* the country away, something has to be done before it's too late."

By now Guy had come to realize that Sir Ronald was not the leader, no one had taken the slightest notice of his arrival.

Guy was at a loss as to who the leader could possibly be. But wait a second, there seemed to be some activity at the entrance people were craning their necks to get a look at what was happening.

The crowd parted and Robert went to the door to greet the newcomers. When he reappeared he was with his mother and father.

Guy had assumed it was the leader who had arrived.

Robert escorted the couple towards Guy.

Sir James shook his hand warmly and Lady Pam kissed his cheek.

Robert took his mother by her hand and said

"Guy, I would like you to meet *the leader*."

Lady Pam the leader! Guy nearly fainted, of all the people she would have been the last one on his list.

She took his arm and manoeuvred him to a quiet part of the room. Every person respectfully made way to give them privacy.

Nemesis

"Did you guess it was me?" she said.

"No I can truthfully say that I would never have guessed in a thousand years."

"Well now you know, I enjoyed our last meeting so much that I claim leader's privilege which means I will visit you once again tonight, is that OK?"

What do you say to a woman who has just stated that she intends to shag your brains out later.

"Does Sir James know about this?"

"He knows and he's content to let someone else take on his duties. He's getting past it in any case."

I'm not surprised thought Guy I'm only half her age and I was shattered after our last bout.

The evening went by in a flash – a buffet dinner and copious amounts of alcohol the conversation increasing in volume fuelled by drink.

Of Lady Pamela there was no sign and he wondered if he had been granted a reprieve, on the other hand if he was honest he had been quite looking forward to bed.

He said goodnight to the group he was with and went upstairs.

He opened the door to his room and found Lady Pam stretched out on the bed stark naked, her legs wide open.

"Don't play hard to get" he said as he stripped off his clothes.

"Don't turn the light off I want to watch" she said.

This time she had no need to help with his erection

Nemesis

the very sight as he had entered the room took care of that.

"Now Guy we have to try as many positions as we can, I'll let you go to sleep if you can manage seven."

He failed by one and they fell asleep competently satisfied. He woke about eight am and felt her kiss him.

God I hope she doesn't want another one. The woman is insatiable.

"I think I'll keep you as my personal stud" she said as she stepped into the shower.

He could barely look Sir James in the face, not to mention Robert. God knows what they thought about the goings on.

After breakfast he excused himself and set out for the long drive to Yorkshire. The traffic on the M1 was horrendous as usual with 50 mile per hour stretches nearly all the way.

He arrived home at 2pm in a foul temper because the journey had taken so long.

I hope Lulu doesn't feel like sex tonight … I'll have to plead a headache.

34

Guy contacted Sir John the next morning.

"I have just returned from the meeting in London and I was introduced to the leader at last. I could give you three guesses as to who it is but I am confident you would fail."

"Well Guy don't keep me in suspense any longer tell me now."

"It's Lady Pamela. I was absolutely sure it would be Sir Ronald who incidentally was present but when Robert introduced her as the leader I was dumb struck."

"Well done Guy I'll get the message to Sandra right away. Was everything OK otherwise, no reason to think they suspect you?"

"No everything went well I think they trust me implicitly."

"By all accounts you seem to be well in Guy?"

"Funny you should use that phrase Sir, you would not believe what I had to do to keep my cover intact."

"Don't like the sound of that. What did you have to do?"

"Well it seems Lady Pam views me as a sex object and I know a gentleman should never divulge matters of this kind but in a nutshell I had to sleep with her. But sleep was the last thing I got."

Nemesis

"All I can say Guy is some have all the luck. You did not confess all to Lulu I hope?"

"No, but should I do you think? I don't like to deceive my wife but there was nothing I could do without causing suspicion."

"Look at it this way, do you tell Lulu that you have killed someone when you return from a mission? No. And I'll tell you another thing, when I was in the game we had women operatives who worked undercover and in many cases they had to have sex with men they couldn't stand in order to protect their legend."

Guy could see the sense in what Sir John had said, and the fact that he had told his wife's father somehow made it seem more honest.

A few days at home was just what he needed, to carry out simple tasks and not have the constant worry of letting something slip.

They went riding on the moor and visited Leeds to shop. Lulu enjoyed his company and prayed for the day when he could be with her always.

Guy was sat in his office when the phone rang, it was he noticed the one supplied by MI5, so he knew it was Sir John.

"Hello Guy, just to keep you in the loop. I passed the news on to Sandra and she is as surprised as us to find Lady Pamela is the big chief. She feels that we, meaning *you*, really should try to catch her in some involvement serious enough to put her away. The British First party is illegal but so far they have done nothing except spout a lot of hot air. That in itself could lead to a prosecution but a smart lawyer would see that they walked away with a smack on the wrist. What we need is something serious where we could put the leaders away for years."

"What about Thompson, surely that's a serious matter?"

"I agree but we would have to prove it was her who ordered the hit. Sir Ronald would be the one doing time."

"Well I will do my best but I'll bet she never gives a direct order. It's based on the cell system."

35

Several weeks went by without any contact. Then a telephone call.

"Hello Guy. Robert speaking. Could you come down to London on Friday? We are expecting a visit from some like minded people in Germany and Poland. The idea being to form a brotherhood right across Europe, it will include France Italy and Hungary and many more in time.?"

"Yes count me in. Where will the meeting be?"

"Not sure but I'll meet you at Kings Cross, take the nine o'clock from Leeds."

"OK, Robert see you on Friday."

Guy considered the implications and did not like it one bit, never before had the destination been kept secret, he decided to share his concern with Sir John.

"Don't like it Guy, as you say you are going to an unknown address and if they *do* suspect something you'll be on your own."

"Look Guy, I'll get back to you in the next few minutes, I'm going to call Sandra."

He rang back in fifteen minutes.

"Sandra is of the same opinion,she feels something's not quite right, she has suggested that you wear a tracker which will tell us where you are. Are you OK with that?"

Nemesis

"Yes I think that's the only thing we can do, might be worrying unnecessarily, it could be just a matter of security to protect the visitors."

*

Friday morning at Kings Cross, Robert was standing by the gate, he shook hands and smiled.

"Hello Guy, good journey?"

They went across to the car park where Robert's car was standing.

"The meeting is at one of our safe houses but when we have visitors from Europe we always take extra care in case special branch follows them."

Robert drove into Canary Wharfe and entered the underground garage of a block of luxury apartments.

They took the lift to the pent house commanding breathtaking views of the river.

"This is rather nice Robert, I wonder how much one of these costs?"

"*Millions* Guy, property prices in London are a joke. You do right to live where you do. If it wasn't for my job I would be with you."

They sat at a glass topped coffee table and Fiona appeared bearing tea and sandwiches.

"Hello Guy, nice to see you again, Sir Ronald will be with us shortly he's bringing our guests."

She poured the tea and then returned to the kitchen.

Guy drank his tea and turned to Robert who had suddenly grown another head. He blinked his eyes, the

Nemesis

room was spinning and he was falling until everything went black.

Guy came to slowly, he realized he was naked and tied firmly to a chair which was fixed to the floor. Robert was sat in a chair facing him and there were two shaven headed toughs standing to each side.

"Welcome back Guy you seem to have dropped off. Just to put you in the picture, we are no longer in the apartment by the river and your tracker which we found quite easily we fixed to the back of a van and could be anywhere by now. I have some questions which I strongly advise you answer truthfully. If you don't, you will suffer and in the end you will tell everybody does. So hear we go, *who do you work for?*"

"I thought I worked for you."

This resulted in a punch administered by one of the apes to his stomach.

"Right, you get the idea now. *WHO do you work for?*"
Guy said

"What makes you think I work for anybody?"

Another blow to his body.

"Well just a shot in the dark how many people do you know who have a tracking device on them? Oh and another thing..." said Robert "...who do you recognise in this photograph?"

He held it up to Guy and then it became clear — *Thompson!*

Guy thought I might have guessed that he would not

keep his side of the bargain.

"This is the man who you killed by hitting him with a stolen car. He looks remarkably well to me. How many others have you lied about?"

"I can answer truthfully, *none*."

"You are in a very bad place Guy, no one can help you because they don't know where you are. You are going to die it's just a matter of will it be quick … or slow and painful? We have all the time in the world, so I'm going now. These fellows will beat you up because they like doing that, I'll come back later and see if you have decided to be sensible."

He walked out and the beating started, mostly on his body. He thought his ribs were broken.

After a while they stopped and left him alone. He considered his options. They were nil, he could hang on and refuse to answer but Robert was right, it was only a matter of time.

The door opened and he prepared himself for more beating, but it was Sir James and Lady Pam.

"We are so disappointed in you Guy, you could have had it all."

"I think I did have it all Sir James, she was one of the best I ever had."

Lady Pam slapped him hard across his face.

"When they come back I want to watch you suffer YOU BASTARD."

Nemesis

Footsteps and then the door opened, Robert entered.

"Have you had a change of mind yet or do I bring the boys in again? Wait a bit I have a better idea, I'll send the boys to bring your wife down here. After they strip her and take turns you might decide to talk sense. Course when they pick her up they're bound to try her out but you never know, she might like it."

With that Robert walked out of the room. A few minutes later the two goons returned and a systematic beating began – this time it was his face.

The door opened once more and the person walked up to Guy grabbed his hair and lifted his battered face to the light. *Marcia*.

"They have made a mess of you lover boy, mother told me all about your nights of passion … mother and daughter you must be proud."

She stepped back and then hit him with a back handed blow to his battered face, this brought laughter from the two apes.

"Sorry, did that *hurt* Guy?"

She bent down and kissed his cheek and at the same time put something in his hand without the two roughs seeing.

"Well I don't suppose I'll see you again Guy so all the best. Take care."

And she was gone.

Nemesis

The skinheads decided that it was time for a break so after a couple of blows to his face they left the basement.

Guy felt the object Marcia had passed to him, it was a safety razor. He manoeuvred his hand until he could start to cut the rope. *Don't drop it* he prayed.

He felt the rope parting and suddenly his hand was free, the other hand still tied but not for long, now the ankles.

The rope fell away and he was free. *Right you bastards!*

He heard footsteps outside and moved so he stood back against the wall on the door's hinged side.

They entered the room and stood shocked as they saw the empty chair. The Israeli martial arts is called Krav Maga. It has one purpose only and that is to kill. In the seconds that they took to realize he had gone, both were dead.

He searched their pockets and found a bunch of keys and stuck in their waistbands two Glock 9mm pistols, he checked the magazines – both fully loaded. He stripped the clothes off the dead guards and dressed in seconds The trainers were a size big but would do. He was out of the door and up a staircase to the ground floor. It took only a moment to realize he was in Sir James' house. One he knew well.

Gun in hand he moved towards the library.

He stopped and listened. Yes he heard voices.

He opened the door a crack and saw all three, Sir James, Robert and Lady Pam.

Nemesis

There was no sign of Marcia and as far as he could tell the three were the only ones present. A slight sound to his rear alerted him and turning he came face to face with Walters the butler who had a large knife raised in his right hand.

Guy grabbed his wrist and spun Walters around so that he crashed through the door into the room.

All three sprang to their feet as Walters unable to keep his balance fell to the floor, the knife slipping out of his hand.

"Good afternoon everyone" said Guy kicking the knife out of reach and pointing the gun. "Sit back down and keep your hands where I can see them."

Walters rose to his feet and Guy beckoned him to join the others.

Recovering her composure Lady Pamela said

"Well what now? There are four of us and one of you."

Guy looked at Robert and said

"Just remind me again what you had planned for my wife?"

And with that he shot Robert right between the eyes.

"Now let's see, there's only three of you now by my reckoning."

"You won't get away with that!" snarled Pam. "We all witnessed that you shot an unarmed man who posed no threat."

"So I did" said Guy, "and by the time I finish here

there will be no one to witness anything. You are all scum and I intend to kill you all."

With that he fired one shot into the head of Sir James.

"Now. I think you are beginning to see how this will end. No one is going to be brought to trial."

Suddenly Walters flung himself at Guy in a vain attempt to get the gun. He made it halfway before he took a 9mm round in the throat.

"That leaves just you and me Leader, I'll give you one chance to survive. Open your safe and give me the names of all your members. I should point out that we will get them in any case, but I would prefer you to hand them over."

"And if I do, you promise that you won't kill me?"

"Yes if you give me all the information you have I promise I won't shoot you."

She led the way upstairs to the main bedroom and moved a catch on an oil painting which swung outwards revealing a wall safe. She entered the combination and the door opened.

"There, all the names are in that little black book."

He quickly scanned through the pages to make sure, he recognized some of the people he had met and then slipped the book into his pocket.

"Now let me go I did what you asked and I know that as a gentleman you would not lie."

Guy walked up to her and said

"I promised not to *shoot* you and I won't …"

Nemesis

With that he hit her on the bridge of her nose killing her instantly. He then searched the house from top to bottom but could find nothing else which would be of any use. He was suddenly very tired.

He picked up the telephone and dialled Sir John's number.

"You had better get down here, it's all over."

He gave the address and then going to the bedroom he knew so well he fell fast asleep.

36

He woke and looked at his watch, 5.30. It was already dark outside. Sir John had not arrived but he suddenly became aware of the presence of another person.

He raised himself on his elbow and saw Marcia sitting in a chair with a pistol held loosely in her hand.

"Did you *have* to kill them Guy, my mother and father as well as my only brother?"

"I believe I did Marcia, they were evil and would have got away with a short prison sentence. Their politics although extreme were not the problem. It was the other things they did that made me act. As far as I know I might spend the rest of my life in prison for doing what I did but it was worth it. Incidentally thank you for what you did. They would have killed me without your help."

Marcia laid the gun down and started to cry. Guy held her close until she stopped.

"What will you do go back to the job you love?"

"Yes I think so, there will be a lot to sort out here but in time it will be for the best."

"I understand you are married Guy, she's a lucky girl tell me about her."

"Well you have met her, Lucinda is her name, you went riding together, she has had a lot to put up with since we met but with any luck that will change."

Nemesis

There was a loud knocking at the front door, Sir John had arrived at last.

When they entered the library Sir John looked at Guy and said *"Good God are there any more.?"*

"Matter of fact there is. One more upstairs."

"Better start at the beginning and tell me the whole story."

Marcia went to the kitchen to prepare some food. Guy had not had anything for twenty four hours.

Sir John rang Sandra at MI5, and was on the telephone for about an hour.

"Right, a clean up team is on the way Guy, do you think Marcia will cooperate in a cover story?"

"Yes I think she will, she saved my life of that there is no doubt, I think she just wants this nightmare to end."

Marcia packed a suitcase and Sir John dropped her off at an hotel on his way back home. Guy went with him and would stay until the mess had been cleared up. Guy rang and told Lulu that he was at her father's and would be home shortly. He then went to bed and slept for fifteen hours.

Next day Sir John filled him in on progress made involving the disposing of the dead.

"The two goons in the cellar were no problem, Sir James his wife and son were involved in a nasty car accident when the vehicle they were travelling in hit a tree and burst into flames killing the driver and the three passengers."

There were lots of loose ends to be tied, Guy contacted Marcia and offered to help her dispose of the house she had lived in her entire life. She thanked him but said she had already put the house on the market and that she was returning to work.

*

Sir John and Guy had a meeting with Sandra at Thames House. They assembled in her suite and over coffee they went over the whole business from start to finish.

"Let me start by telling you that Sir Ronald and Fiona were arrested yesterday. They will be charged with treason, which is the most serious charge they can face. The leader of the opposition has on my advice called Thompson in for a talk and told him that all promises made to him are cancelled owing to his failure to keep his side of he bargain. He threatened to go public but soon changed his mind when it was pointed out to him that his actions would have caused your death if not for Marcia. She, incidentally, knew nothing about her parents and brother being the brains behind the British First Party. The first she knew was when she arrived home and discovered that you were being held prisoner.

It only remains for me to thank you Guy for your action in bringing an end to this dangerous party. As it's a *black operation* you will not receive any public recognition, but unofficially the Prime Minister has asked me to convey his thanks. Now I'm sure you're ready for a long rest and perhaps a well earned holiday, but there will be a position for you in MI5 if you want it. This time official."

Guy thanked her for all she had done and said he would think about her offer.

"After all, I'm too young to retire."

Then it was home to his wife. They celebrated with a dinner for two and an excellent vintage red courtesy of MI5. He told Lulu everything (except the Lady Pamela episode). He said how Marcia had rescued him, and confessed to the killing of six people.

Lulu said

"I knew you were involved in something dangerous and that you were unable to talk about it but I never imagined the danger you were in."

"MI5 have offered me a job if I want it, but this time it's all above board, no more sleepless nights."

"After we have had a good long holiday we will talk about that again Guy, but for the present all I want is for you to take me to bed."

THE END

Acknowledgements

My thanks to my wife, Sheila, for her support;
and to Carol for her technical advice and encouragement.

To Beth
with best wishes

Brian